SPECIAL MESSAGE TO READERS

THE ULVERSCROFT FOUNDATION
(registered UK charity number 264873)
was established in 1972 to provide funds for research, diagnosis and treatment of eye diseases. Examples of major projects funded by the Ulverscroft Foundation are:-

- The Children's Eye Unit at Moorfields Eye Hospital, London
- The Ulverscroft Children's Eye Unit at Great Ormond Street Hospital for Sick Children
- Funding research into eye diseases and treatment at the Department of Ophthalmology, University of Leicester
- The Ulverscroft Vision Research Group, Institute of Child Health
- Twin operating theatres at the Western Ophthalmic Hospital, London
- The Chair of Ophthalmology at the Royal Australian College of Ophthalmologists

You can help further the work of the Foundation by making a donation or leaving a legacy. Every contribution is gratefully received. If you would like to help support the Foundation or require further information, please contact:

THE ULVERSCROFT FOUNDATION
The Green, Bradgate Road, Anstey
Leicester LE7 7FU, England
Tel: (0116) 236 4325

website: www.foundation.ulverscroft.com

ONE SUMMER WEEKEND

Alicia Marlowe's life as an executive coach is well under control — until she meets her new client, Jack Smith. Jack's reputation precedes him, and Alicia knows immediately that he spells trouble. Not least because he reminds her of someone else — a man who broke her heart and made her resolve never to lower her guard again. As long as she keeps Jack in his place, Alicia thinks she might just make it through unscathed. But Jack has other ideas — including a 'business' trip to the Lake District . . .

JULIET ARCHER

ONE SUMMER WEEKEND

Complete and Unabridged

LINFORD
Leicester

First published in Great Britain in 2018 by
Ruby Fiction
an imprint of Choc Lit Limited
Surrey

First Linford Edition
published 2019
by arrangement with
Choc Lit Limited
Surrey

A catalogue record for this book is available from the British Library.

ISBN 978–1–4448–4003–2

For those on a journey

Acknowledgements

A big thank you to:

Gordon, Sarah, Will and Chelsea, Mike and Jo, Elizabeth, Jo and Neil.

The Choc Lit and Ruby Fiction family for their continuing support, and Tasting Panel members Jo O, Toos H, Margaret M, Janet S, Jo L, Melissa C, Samantha E, Susan D, Christina G, Hilary B, Ruth N, Steph P and Jenny K.

C19 members for their encouragement of a much earlier version of this story.

Elizabeth Gaskell, for her *North & South* inspiration.

1

I marched out into the metallic heat of the car park, summoned the scattered shreds of my professional detachment and branded a promise into my brain.

Never. Ever. Again.

I should have known it would be a wasted journey. My client comfort zone was male, middle-aged and middle-class. Only the first of these applied to the Chief Executive of Leo Components, major employer in the shrunken Lancashire mill town of Grimshaw: Jack Smith — industrial magnate and, if the local tabloids were to be believed, 'babe magnet of the North West' in his spare time.

Oh yes, I'd done my pre-meeting research — and not just in the *Financial Times* archives. I'd found only limited information on Leo Components, privately owned and rumoured to be heading for a Stock Market flotation. But there'd been plenty about 'Jack the Lad' — and I'd only looked at the last few months' media coverage.

At thirty-six years old he was hardly middle-aged; and Adam Chesterfield, the mutual contact who'd recommended my services, had described him as a self-made man from humble beginnings. I could have predicted, then, that this first meeting would be more challenging than most. I just hadn't anticipated the scale of the challenge, nor the nature of it.

No, I reflected as I unlocked my car, this . . . creature was not in the usual mould at all. The managing directors I'd coached so far were father, even grandfather, figures; weathered captains of industry, with an appreciation of how executive coaching would help them succeed in the modern business world. Men I could take out of their little compartments, dust down a bit and put back with the sense of a job well done.

And at least they gave me the *right*

kind of undivided attention, whereas he . . . But it was all academic; I would not be coaching him. There was more chance of me running naked through the streets of Grimshaw.

Which was probably what he'd been imagining as soon as I'd walked into his office.

Now for the long drive south; at least I would beat the Friday afternoon rush. I wrenched off my jacket, hurled it onto the back seat along with my beautiful new Aspinal laptop bag, and settled myself behind the wheel. Instead of starting the engine, however, I glared across the car park at the drab 1960s-style building I'd just left and, against my better judgement, relived the past hour.

I had to admit, those tabloid photos of Jack Smith hadn't done him justice. In the flesh, his build was leaner, his face younger, his eyes more . . . predatory. His handshake was business-like and brief, but the impression of his interested surprise lingered.

'So you're Alicia Marlowe, from Coaches for Growth.' Voice like black velvet over gravel, with an understated northern accent that other women would probably find very attractive.

He went on, 'From what Adam said, I thought you'd be a lot older.' A pause, while his gaze travelled up and down. 'I might have to ask you to show me your credentials.' And then I had his smile to contend with, wide and wicked, inviting me to respond in the same suggestive vein.

I gave him a look of stone. 'If you need proof of my professional qualifications, I'm sure that can be arranged.' A deliberate glance at my watch. 'We have a lot to discuss. Let's get this meeting under way.'

Still grinning, he gestured to a pair of vast black leather armchairs. I swept past him in my navy suit, tailored white shirt and sensible heels. I'd never had to think of them as protective armour — until now.

We sat at opposite sides of a low table

whose gleaming glass top was engraved with a rampant lion: the Leo Components logo and a symbol of outdated sexism, very much like its Chief Executive. But I counted to ten, accepted the offer of coffee, took my laptop from my bag and located the file named 'Jack Smith — On-boarding Meeting'. To avoid any small talk, I busied myself with typing a few extra headings for some much-needed structure. I was aware of him fidgeting with his phone; making arrangements for tonight's conquest, no doubt.

As soon as his PA — more mature and homely than I'd expected — brought the coffee, I fixed my blandest smile in place and opened the dialogue. 'I'm here at Adam's request. What do you think he had in mind when he recommended you for coaching?'

He had the sense to pocket his phone before I was tempted to confiscate it. 'Haven't a clue. He's a devious old bugger — as you'll know, from the happy times you spent coaching him.'

A golden opportunity to introduce one of the ground rules. 'I'm afraid I don't disclose personal information about my clients, past or present, least of all to other clients. Or should I say prospective ones.'

His gaze slipped to the collar of my high-necked shirt. 'Now you mention it, I can't imagine you disclosing anything to anyone.'

My smile faded. He was being just ambiguous enough to discourage accusations of inappropriate behaviour. Why was I wasting my time here? Doing Adam a favour simply wasn't worth it.

As if reading my mind, he raised his eyes to my face. Not a glimmer of apology, more the defiant bravado of a naughty schoolboy. He said, 'Look, round here an executive coach is a bus with air-conditioning or a toilet, both if you're lucky. But Adam thinks I need one, and he reckons you're one of the best.'

'Which takes us back to my original question.' I managed to retrieve my smile. 'What do you think he had in mind when he suggested you might benefit from coaching?'

He took a gulp of coffee, then ran the back of his hand across his forehead. Long fingers, no wedding ring — naturally. 'Oh, I suppose the obvious answer is that the company's just taken over a larger competitor, Sphinx Industries. It'll be a lot of graft bringing Sphinx into line, but of course I'm up for it.'

'I see.' I typed *Domineering management style, arrogant belief in own abilities*. Normally I kept my notes neutral and observation-based, but Jack Smith deserved the special accolade of an instant diagnosis. 'What's the not-so-obvious answer?'

'Does there have to be one?'

'Are you certain there's not?'

He shifted in his seat; restless energy, or a rare moment of self-awareness? 'I've never run a business of that size before. And I can't afford to make a mistake.'

Ah, now we were getting somewhere.

Uses aggression to mask his fear of failure. 'And how do you feel about being coached?'

'Don't know what to expect. All I can say is — I'm not used to being told what to do. Except by my mother, who still treats me like a five-year-old.'

I sidestepped the personal reference. 'At Coaches for Growth, we don't believe in a directive approach — it's all about empowerment.'

He had the nerve to laugh, a deep-throated chuckle that filled the room. 'You can call it whatever you want, as long as it helps me work smarter. I couldn't work much harder.'

Or play any harder, according to the media coverage; but I let that pass. 'To summarise, then, you could say that the aim of your coaching would be to increase your confidence levels and emotional intelligence in a dynamic corporate environment, in order to work more effectively at integrating your recent acquisition?'

The chuckle expanded into a shout

of laughter. 'I couldn't say that at all! Looks like we're going to need a third person at these sessions to bloody well translate — is that why you charge such a high fee? We'd better change to payment by results.'

'The fee is non-negotiable,' I said stiffly, 'and doesn't include a translator — although you're welcome to provide one at your own expense. Are you saying you disagree with the aim of the coaching?'

'No, but you might need to help me with some of those long words.'

I added *Childish sense of humour* and said briskly, 'How will you know you've achieved the agreed aim?'

'Easy — the Board and I have set some ambitious targets. By the end of this financial year, that's the thirty-first of March, we need to have increased our sales across the two companies by fifteen per cent, same with profit before tax, and trimmed the workforce by ten per cent. Typical stuff to justify the cost of buying a bigger company. But to do all that I'll need to become more effective from today. Actually, make that yesterday.'

This was more like it. I made a note of the targets, folded my hands in my lap and launched into a well-rehearsed routine. 'End of March, that's just under ten months from now. I would normally suggest working with you over a six-month period. More frequent meetings to begin with, then monthly sessions, provided we're making satisfactory progress. In theory, that fits in with your timescale. But you must understand that, although the start and end points in coaching are predetermined, the middle part, what I call the journey, is intangible, very much an unknown quantity. Not like a journey by plane or by train, where everything is scheduled. And, if my suspicions are correct, your personality type will find this concept rather difficult. You like things to be quantifiable, like your Board targets.'

'How else do I know I'm on track?'

'Quite. But there is no track in the coaching journey, you're forging your own path with an experienced coach as your guide. Of course, you know where you want to be, what your end point looks like — '

'I should hope so, at my age.' No sign of that smile, just the taunt still there in his voice.

I finished with a frosty, ' — but there's plenty of unfamiliar territory along the way.'

'I'll bet. How would it work, then?' He leaned back in his chair and stared at me through half-closed eyes, as if . . . well, as if thinking about something else entirely. Or was that *my* over-active imagination, provoked by his permanent state of innuendo?

I willed my blushes away and focused on a picture just over his left shoulder, a surprisingly tasteful watercolour of a slate-grey lake surrounded by snow-capped hills. 'We would start with an intense period of two or three days finding out about you, seeing how you interact at work, attending one of your management meetings, understanding your personality, and so on. Then there are various options. You can go for remote coaching, by Skype or video conference, but you would be less likely to achieve your aim within the required timescale. Or you can come to our offices in Helsingham, just off the M3, for face-to-face meetings. Clients often find they get more out of coaching if they're removed from everyday distractions. Or our coach can come here, which will enable him to observe — '

'Him?' He leaned in, frowning. 'I thought it was going to be you?'

I didn't answer immediately. Although I hadn't intended to say 'him' instead of 'me', that simple slip of the tongue presented a relatively painless way out of my dilemma. Times were tough, and we couldn't afford to lose this business. But if I handed this assignment to one of my male colleagues . . . Let's just say that Jack Smith would find his masculine wiles eliminated from the agenda,

Coaches for Growth would get its profit — and I could return to my comfort zone.

I leaned forward too, a controlled display of assertiveness. Up close, his blue eyes showed flecks of green. And they were a lot less friendly than before. 'I'm afraid I'll have to think very carefully about taking you on as a client.' As I said this, as I finally expressed my reservations to his face, I felt a thrill of relief run through me. I continued, warming to my theme, 'The relationship between coach and coachee is built on rapport, openness and trust — and for me there's something not right about the way we're interacting. Equally, I suggest you give some thought to whether *you* could work with *me*.'

He drew away, the frown deepening into a scowl. 'I didn't realise this was a bloody dating agency. 'Male, six foot two, aged thirty-six, good sense of humour, would like to meet female, aged — well, I'd put you in your late twenties, for *executive coaching*?' I don't think so! This is a business transaction, pure and simple. I buy your services, you send me an invoice and I pay it in thirty days, regardless of your terms. End of story.'

He might be right about my age, but he was wrong about everything else. 'Coaching's a very personal service — '

'So's a dating agency — '

'I'd rather use the analogy of a doctor,' I said, in desperation; not an ideal metaphor, perhaps, but too late now. 'Do you prefer a male doctor, or a female one, or doesn't it matter? Do you want someone who's directive, or consultative? Do you like a lot of bed-side manner, or as little superfluous interaction as possible?' As soon as I said that last sentence, I regretted it. I added coolly, 'There are so many factors to consider at this level of coaching.'

'My ideal doctor's female and consultative, with a great bedside manner and warm hands. When it comes to coaching, though, does it matter whether I'm a man and you're a woman?'

Another time — another place — another man, saying the same words. The skeleton of a past life stirred, and I shrank back in my seat. 'I think we should change the subject.'

He raised an eyebrow. 'But isn't coaching the subject here? What else would you like to talk about?'

Sip the coffee . . . force the smile. 'Let me discuss this assignment with my colleagues. We may decide that you'd benefit more from having a different coach.'

'But I want *you*.'

That was when it hit me. Maybe everything in this ill-judged meeting had been building up to this moment, like the script for a nightmare. This man, with his invading eyes and soft-spoken intent, had pushed my life into rewind. Back three years to a Californian summer, when another man had said the words, '*But I want* you.' So many times, in so many ways. '*But I want you, Aleesha*.' 'I *want* you.' And the worst insult of all, '*I love you, Aleesha. I always will*.'

Back then, I had been totally unprepared. But not this time. This time I was ready, and I would deal with it. Fight it. Finish it before it could even begin.

Try to breathe . . . swallow . . . move on. The words almost stuck in my throat. 'We can't always have what we want.'

'You sound like my bloody mother. Except she says 'I want never gets'. Up north we have no sense of grammar.'

Take control . . . take control. 'Of course, cultural differences can be a fascinating source of study in their own right, but they will also materially inform the dynamics of the coach-coachee relationship.'

Silence, while he took this in, followed by a full-bodied laugh. 'I can feel my vocabulary getting bigger by the minute.'

That did it. I remembered to save the file, then slammed the laptop into my bag, careless of its pristine sky-blue lining. 'I'll email you on Monday with our decision.' Grim-faced, I stood up and jabbed out my hand; a business reflex, nothing more.

He swung easily to his feet and trapped my hand in his, eyes exploring mine. I wanted to snatch my hand and my gaze away, but I couldn't. It was three years since I'd felt like this — a butterfly on the point of a pin. Beneath its protective armour, my heart thumped and reeled.

He said, 'Let's hope it's the right decision. For both of us.' And something in his look . . . as if somehow he *knew*.

Which meant it was even more important to find a way out of this assignment — and fast.

2

On Monday I was in the office for eight o'clock. It had been a weekend of self-distraction — with only limited success. A trip to the gym, the first in a while, to punish my mind through my body. An evening with a couple of friends, both first-time mothers whose babies dominated the conversation even when tucked up in bed. A long Skype call with my parents, including an inch-by-inch survey of their new retirement villa in Spain. Cleaning the flat, which turned into a physical workout on a par with the gym.

In the end, it was a relief to go to work. As I drove through the business park on the grassy outskirts of Helsingham, I couldn't help contrasting its flowering shrubs and fountains with the concrete wastes of Grimshaw. What chance did people have of functioning effectively when they were surrounded by ugliness? Not that this excused Jack Smith's behaviour in the slightest, but the view from his office window must be a lot more depressing than mine.

I knew that my director, Stuart Carson, would already be at his desk. It was usually worth gauging the depth of his Monday gloom and checking whether it had been sweetened by his morning latte. But the need to exorcise Jack Smith from my life had been gnawing at me all weekend, and I wanted to get this interview over.

The door of Stuart's room was closed; always a bad sign. Either he'd been landed with entertaining the kids on Sunday, or he'd overdone the nineteenth hole at the golf club. I gave a firm knock and entered without waiting for an answer. As I clicked the door shut behind me, he looked up from his iPad. Grey face, bloodshot eyes — a nineteenth-hole extravaganza, obviously; and I suspected he'd barely touched his latte.

'Just a quick update on Leo Components,' I said brightly.

'Is the contract signed?'

'Not yet, but — '

'That's not like you. It was the on-boarding meeting on Friday, wasn't it? Is there a problem?'

'Possibly.'

He sighed and folded his arms above the rounded summit of his stomach. 'You'd better sit down and tell me what's going on.'

Which I did, more or less. As I had no intention of jeopardising my career prospects, I gave him an abridged version of my meeting and omitted certain facts entirely. Like how Jack Smith had succeeded in reintroducing me to the darkest moments from my past and prompted my first anxiety attack in at least two years.

Stuart reached for his latte. 'So he eyed you up and said things that had a double meaning? Are you telling me that's never happened to you in a coaching situation?'

'Never.' An automatic response that consigned the past to a sealed container, gathering dust; until my meeting last Friday, it wouldn't even have registered as a lie.

'Perhaps with older clients you don't tend to notice — '

'I've never had a problem with *any* of our clients.' That much was true; the . . . incident had happened before I joined Coaches for Growth.

'I should hope not.' Then, peering into his coffee cup, 'But does that mean they never think about you in that way? What I'm trying to say is, if you're not expecting to see something then you won't necessarily see it.' As he shifted his gaze to my face, I quickly masked my astonishment. What the hell was he implying? He continued, 'Whereas you were gunning for this Smith guy before you'd even met him. What was it you said last week? He can't appear in public without a semi-naked woman draped over him, or words to that effect.'

Two challenges here, both unanticipated. I took refuge in a dismissive laugh and tackled the first one head on. 'Why would Gerald Foster *ever* think about me in that way? Or Adam Chesterfield? Or Tom Rigg? They're happily married, as far as I can tell.'

'Jeez, Alicia! Happily married men still look at other women, especially young and very attractive ones. It's just that most of them do nothing more than look.'

I frowned at the gleaming oak floor. Even if I didn't believe him, the damage had been done; the memory of those pleasant, fatherly clients had now acquired a sinister quality. As for Stuart himself, who would pass for happily married on a good day and who'd just implied that he thought I was very attractive . . . I risked a glance at him, fearing a Jack Smith moment. Instead of catching him in mid-leer, I found him slurping at his latte; the relief was overwhelming.

He drained his cup and threw it in

the bin beside him. 'How did you leave things at Leo Components?'

At last we were approaching decision time. 'I said I'd consult my colleagues to agree who would be the most appropriate coach, and that I'd email him with the outcome today.'

He fingered his iPad, as if bored with our conversation. 'And when does he want the coaching to start?'

'As soon as possible.'

'Really?' That claimed his full attention; I could almost hear the cogs in his brain whirring. He went on, 'The initial payment would certainly help our cash flow, get us out of a temporary hole.' He paused, and mustered an expression of sympathetic concern. 'Look — if you've really got a problem with him, I can find someone else. Just not immediately. If, on the other hand, you could start him off, do the deep dive stage . . . Not ideal to switch coaches part way, but the contract covers a certain amount of flexibility. Of course, you'll have supervision available to you

— Judy's the one you prefer, isn't she? — and I'll get a replacement coach lined up — probably Gary when he's back from holiday in July. But remember it's your choice.'

And, at Coaches for Growth, that meant taking full responsibility for the consequences. I closed my eyes, visualising the decision as a fork in an unfamiliar road. My instinctive preference was for the wide, smooth path that snaked confidently into the distance; in other words, refuse the assignment, hope that the company would still secure the business after a few weeks' delay and focus on coaching within my self-appointed boundaries.

Except that the boundaries were no longer as clear-cut as I'd believed; Stuart's feedback suggested I'd been unobservant and naïve about my previous clients. Which meant that this was building into a professional issue as well as a personal one. If I took this path, I suspected that it would ultimately bring me back to where I was now.

My other option was a thicket of bramble bushes with no obvious way through, and I had no idea where I would end up: high risk for an uncertain reward. On the other hand, I reasoned, the risk was for a limited time only, with an external supervisor to provide professional guidance. I could even ask her to observe the coaching sessions in person; that should keep Jack Smith in his place.

But I needed to cover off every eventuality. 'I'll take the assignment,' I said slowly, 'on one condition — that I can opt out at any stage, if I feel it's necessary.'

For the first time since I'd entered his room, Stuart smiled. 'Agreed, but only because you're not usually this high-maintenance. Thanks, Alicia, and keep me posted.'

I went out of his room before I said something I'd regret. High-maintenance? A knee-jerk reaction to the fact that — for once — I wouldn't be bringing the business home at minimum cost and disruption. Operating within my client comfort zone — with a low level of supervision — produced the biggest profit for Coaches for Growth, time after time. But that didn't mean it should be taken for granted. In fact, nothing in coaching should be taken for granted, as I knew only too well.

When I returned to my desk, I decided to 'keep Stuart posted' by sending him a very detailed record of our conversation, with a request for a definition of 'high-maintenance' that I could share with HR; that should keep him on his toes. Next, I looked up the most expensive hotel within twenty miles of Grimshaw, and found a superior de luxe room, whatever that entailed, at a gratifyingly high price. Finally, I turned my attention to the paperwork for Leo Components, a straightforward matter of inserting the client details in the designated places and, as always, checking the small print.

Just as I was saving the files, an email pinged into my inbox. From Jack

Smith, with 'Change of Heart' as the subject line. I had to read the short message several times before it sank in.

Dear Alicia
Thank you for coming to Grimshaw last Friday. I have thought about our meeting and decided not to take the executive coaching any further.
Rgds
Jack

Oh, really? We'd see about *that*.

I dialled the mobile number in his email signature. One ring, two rings . . .

A curt, 'Yes?' Did he actually know who was calling, or was he always this abrupt on the phone?

'Good morning, it's Alicia Marlowe.'

The smallest of pauses. 'You got my email?'

'I did, but — '

'I was going to ring you, actually — to apologise for Friday.' No black-velvet voice today; he obviously didn't like apologising.

And I didn't like being wrong-footed. 'Apologise for what exactly?' I couldn't help sounding belligerent; after all, there were so many moments to choose from.

He gave a humourless laugh. 'From what Adam said . . . well, I got the impression you were an old battleaxe. I wasn't expecting you to be so . . . ' A tantalising pause; then, 'Look, I'm sorry if I made you feel uncomfortable. Don't know what got into me.'

'Thank you for that, at least.' I wrote '*Games?*' on the pad in front of me. 'On to other matters — I was rather surprised by your email.'

'I only did what you said and thought about it carefully. Why would you find that surprising?'

I crossed out the question mark after '*Games?*' again and again, until it was obliterated. Then I said, with far more composure than I felt, 'What specifically is preventing you from going ahead?'

Silence. At last he came out with, 'I don't think I'll be able to put in the hours. And the money's a bit steep.'

Even he didn't sound convinced by such lame excuses, and I took full advantage. 'Don't you think you'll recoup the hours and the money several times over, in terms of increased effectiveness and improved business performance? I can provide you with well-researched evidence that good coaching yields a return of six to ten times the initial investment.'

'I'm sure you can. But I don't need good coaching — I need the best, which according to Adam is you. And you more or less told me on Friday that you wouldn't coach me.'

'What if I told you that I'd had a change of heart too?'

More silence.

'Of course,' I continued, 'we'll need to agree some ground rules about what is and isn't appropriate, in relation to behaviour or subjects for discussion. And I may invite a third person to our sessions.' I tried not to make it sound like a threat.

'A translator? Or a referee?' Oh, *now* the black velvet was back, swathes of it.

'The latter — someone to remind you of the rules,' I said coldly. 'I'll email you this morning with a contract and confidentiality agreement to sign and return, as well as our initial invoice — to be paid within the stated terms, please. There'll also be some questionnaires to complete and send back before our first session. Talking of which, have you got your diary to hand? We'll need a couple of days so that I can observe you in your working environment. They should include a formal meeting with your management team and a visit to an external stakeholder, preferably a key customer.'

A series of muffled taps and curses from the other end of the phone; then, 'The next management team meeting's a week on Thursday at ten o'clock, and I can set up a customer visit for the Friday.'

I checked my diary. 'That's fine, I'll come to your office for nine o'clock a week on Thursday.'

'It's a date. Do you need me to book a hotel?'

An unfortunate juxtaposition, as though — in his sordid little mind, at any rate — one thing would inevitably lead to the other. Deliberately done, of course, to undermine my professional approach. 'Yes, the twenty-first of June is certainly a date according to my calendar. And no thanks, I'll make my own hotel arrangements — '

He cut in with, 'Is Thursday the twenty-first? How the hell — ?' A moment's hesitation before he rushed on, his voice low and charged with anger, as if reprimanding himself. 'I was going to have the day off and get Betsy to move the meeting to the following week . . . Serves me right for not checking . . . Too bloody late now!'

I tried to make sense of this sudden confession — and failed. 'Is there a problem with that date?'

A distinctly audible release of breath. 'Only that it's my father's sixty-fifth birthday — at least, it would have been if he was still here. He should have been celebrating his retirement, but instead . . .' He stopped, as if lost in his own thoughts.

'Instead?' I prompted. Nothing more than professional curiosity: if whatever had happened to his father was affecting his work performance, we would need to deal with it.

'Forget it,' he said, brusquely.

I waited, but he obviously felt he'd shared enough. We ended the call with a tentative agreement to talk again — once he'd had a chance to look at the documents and fix up the customer visit. Then I sent him our standard email with the Leo Components files attached, and stored his number in my phone contacts. Not because I envisaged dialling it frequently, if at all; more so that I could identify when *he* was ringing *me* — and let it go to voicemail. Here was a man who'd perfected point scoring to the level of an Olympic sport, and I'd need time to prepare for even the simplest conversation.

In fact, for our first session I decided I'd travel to Lancashire by train on the Wednesday and have an extra night at High Stone Hall, the luxury hotel and spa I'd located. That way, I'd be physically and mentally fresh for whatever games he decided to play next.

As I walked to the kitchen to make myself a coffee, something from my earlier conversation with Stuart niggled. '*You were gunning for the guy before you even met him*.'

If that was true, I had my reasons. The brooding good looks, the maverick style, the playboy reputation — Jack Smith could have been Troy Randall Travers' younger brother.

Troy Randall Travers: a chapter of my life I thought I'd ripped out of the book and thrown away. But then . . . wasn't this going to be a coaching journey for me, too?

3

It didn't take long for Jack Smith to be in touch. He acknowledged my email by return and copied in his HR director as requested. To my surprise, he sent through the signed documents and completed the questionnaires by the end of the week. He even paid the invoice within the stipulated term of seven days.

The following Monday morning he rang my mobile and, as planned, I let it go to voicemail. The problem was that he didn't leave a message. This happened several times, but I refused to bend and call him back; not until I knew what he wanted to discuss.

Towards lunch time Celia, our PA, came and perched on the edge of my desk. She was only a few years younger than me, but seemed to live on a different planet. For a start, she regarded her job as an inconvenient break in a chaotic round of dating, shopping and partying. By her standards, I did far too much work and far too little of anything else. I was therefore an object of pity.

But not today, it seemed. She waited for me to finish an email, then pounced. 'This Jack Smith, does he look as good as he sounds on the phone?'

No way was I answering that. She could ask Google — given that she seemed to spend most of her working day surfing the internet. But her question triggered one of my own. 'When did you speak to *him*?'

'A few minutes ago. By the way, he can't understand why you won't answer his calls. Especially, he says, when you earn your living by talking to your clients.'

My lips tightened. 'For all he knows, I could have been in a meeting — '

'Oops! I told him you weren't. But if you want a job swap, *I'll* do the four days with him — '

'Four? I'm only up there for two!'

'Not any more. That's the message he asked me to give you — he's fixed up a customer visit, but the guy's only available over the weekend. Some sort of outdoor activity thingy in the Lake District, and he's wangled you an invitation.'

I digested this information in silence. In the absence of a finalised schedule for the Friday, I'd booked my train ticket as an open return. But the fact that I could travel home on the Sunday without additional expense simply wasn't the point. 'And if I have other plans . . . ?'

'Your diary's blank, I told him you were free.'

We usually blocked out personal commitments in our work diaries, in case we had to travel to Monday morning meetings the night before — or attend coaching conferences, which were often held on a Saturday. Normally, Celia was slow off the mark to establish my availability for anything — except on this occasion.

It turned out that she'd been even

more helpful. She went on, 'He said he hoped he wasn't tearing you away from a nice relaxing weekend with the man in your life, but I told him that you didn't have one.'

For some reason, this rankled even more than the previous revelation. 'In future, please don't share that sort of information with clients,' I said tetchily. 'And before I decide whether I'm going, did you get any details about the weekend?'

'Yeah, the customer's name is Bill McGraw and someone called Mitch McGraw will be there too. Oh, and I wrote down the address of where you're staying . . . Here it is. Blencathra Lodge, Threlkeld. Sounds like a foreign language, doesn't it?'

'A hotel?' I clicked on Google, ready to check the reviews. Or at least confirm that it was a valid address and not some subterfuge on Jack Smith's part. When it came to getting his own way, that man would be capable of anything; abduction was probably the least of my worries . . .

Celia interrupted my train of thought. 'No, I think it's where Bill and Mitch live.'

'Oh. Is anyone else staying with them?'

'Don't know. Anyway, Jack said you'd be out and about most of the time, going up hills and things.'

It sounded as if Bill and Mitch were a couple; at least their company would offer me some protection against Jack Smith. And, as there was no mention of any women, I wouldn't have to watch him hitting on every available female under forty. Nevertheless, I felt uneasy.

'Thank you for the message, Celia, I'll give him a call.'

As soon as she'd dawdled back to her desk, I reached for my mobile and looked up Jack Smith's number. After several controlled breaths, I selected it and waited.

He answered it on the fifth ring. 'Morning, Alicia.' Did he have a photographic memory, or had he stored my number in his phone contacts just as I'd stored his?

'It's afternoon, at least down south.'

'What the — ? You're right, it's past twelve o'clock up here too. Strange to think we're in the same time zone.'

'Amazing. Now, about the deep dive — '

'The what?'

A sudden vision of plunging into the sea, the blue-green-flecked sea, with this man; not side-by-side synchronisation, but a perilous tangle of limbs . . . Yet I'd used the words 'deep dive' regularly in previous client conversations, with no side-effects whatsoever.

I made a mental note to delete the term from my coaching script. 'I meant the two days I've arranged to spend in Grimshaw.'

'Except it's now four days — did Celia tell you?'

'She did, but I need to understand what it involves before I commit.'

'Observing me with a key customer in a working environment. Exactly what you asked for.'

'Do you normally transact business over a weekend in the wilds of the Lake District?'

'With this particular customer, yes.'

'It just seems . . . highly irregular.'

'Do you never do work at the weekend, or meet customers away from the office?'

I was silent.

He went on, silkily, 'Back to what you said earlier. What are we diving into, and how deep?'

Screen the vision out, *and the voice. Focus on the words — except even the words radiate danger* . . . I cleared my throat. 'It's a metaphor for rapid and total . . . immersion in a subject or situation.'

There, I've said it: total immersion. A phrase that awoke an older memory, an older danger, in the Californian sun . . .

Jack was saying, 'So just think how deep our dive'll be if we've got four days instead of two. And we'll be in the ideal place for it. Did you know that

Wastwater is the deepest lake in England, and Windermere the largest? Although we're actually staying near Derwentwater and Bassenthwaite, if you want to look it up on a map.'

Intriguing names, or was it just the lilt of his accent? In spite of myself, I reached for the mouse. In a few clicks my screen was an intricate pattern of blue, brown and green — the usual colour-coded deception. Because 'The map is not the territory.'

I wasn't aware that I'd said it out loud, until he asked, 'What do you mean?'

'Nothing.'

'No, tell me. It sounded like something important.'

A pause, weighing up the risks. 'It's a statement about the relationship between objects and their representation. First time I heard it was when I saw Magritte's painting 'The Treachery of Images' in Los Angeles. Do you know it?'

'No. You're interested in art?'

The question struck me as unnecessarily personal; I ignored it and went on, 'Magritte painted a picture of a pipe with the caption 'This is not a pipe' — except in French, of course — to convey that the painting is merely the image of a pipe, not the pipe itself.'

'What's Los Angeles like?'

Hot and bright and full of treachery. Nothing to do with the painting; I held no grudge against Magritte. Just a pity I hadn't applied his message to the man standing beside me in the gallery . . .

'Hot and bright, that's all I remember.' *Deep breath, move on*. 'To answer your original question — people confuse maps with the underlying territories, just as they confuse models of reality with reality itself. As Joni Mitchell put it, 'It's clouds' illusions I recall, I really don't know clouds at all'.'

'Or love.'

'Excuse me?'

'She said the same about love.'

A non-committal 'Right'; as if I didn't know the song off by heart. Odd that he, too . . . well, I wouldn't have thought he was a Joni Mitchell fan. I continued, 'Now, who will I be meeting at the weekend?'

'I can give you their names and tell you something about them — but, as you've just said, how will that help you deal with the reality?'

Oh, for God's sake! 'Look, I need to prepare.'

'Just make sure you bring the right gear — '

'That wasn't the kind of preparation I meant — '

'Walking boots or heavy shoes, wellies, waterproofs and some warm clothes. You never know with the Lakes, even in summer.'

'I don't know, I've never been.'

An incredulous laugh. 'You've never been to the most beautiful part of England? You 'aven't lived, lass, you 'aven't lived. Lakes and trees and proper hills, not those pimples you have in the South. You'll think it's wonderful, everyone does.'

I said waspishly, 'You'd probably describe Grimshaw as the Venice of the

North simply because it has a canal. So I'll reserve judgement on your lyrical waxings about the Lake District.'

The laugh softened to a chuckle. 'Good to know you've got a sense of humour, even if it is at my expense.' Then, in a more serious tone, 'Is there anything else I need to tell you about the weekend?'

There was — but whether he would be a reliable source of information was debatable. I decided to throw down one last gauntlet, and lowered my voice to a steely whisper. 'I want to make something perfectly clear. If I consider that I'm being put in any sort of compromising situation, I will take appropriate action immediately. Do you understand?'

'Nope. I have a feeling that whatever you think of as compromising I'd call completely reasonable. Let's put it another way: you're safe with me, and you have my word on that.'

Safe? I felt anything but! Despite my attempt to take the moral high ground, he'd out-manoeuvred me. As for him giving me his word, how far could I trust *that*? I brought the call to a close as quickly as I could, and found my gaze flicking back to the map on my computer screen. Blue for water, brown for hills, green for forests — a familiar enough representation; but the territory beneath was totally unknown.

A tingle of anticipation ran down my spine; the thought of seeing the Lake District for the first time, no doubt.

4

At 8.55 a.m. on the twenty-first of June, I was back at Leo Components. This time, however, I arrived by taxi, and fully aware of what I was walking into.

Same business outfit as last time, but I'd had a head-to-toe beauty treatment at the hotel spa the day before. I'd also allowed the stylist to trim my hair; not that it looked any different while in its usual French pleat. The pampering made me feel relaxed and confident, ready for anything Jack Smith could throw at me.

Today the sky was overcast. With no sunlight to burnish it, I was struck by Grimshaw's bleak monochrome: ashen clouds fused with smoke from its chimneys, soot-scarred factory walls reared above murky canal ways. It was as though I'd stepped into a Lowry painting.

This was an industrial heritage that could apparently inspire, however, as well as oppress. The taxi driver took great pride in relating snippets of social history, pointing out where the Victorian mill owners had once lived . . . where local lads had fought Irish migrants for work . . . where a series of strikes had brought down the last of the textile manufacturers.

Absorbed in a bygone age, I found that the last part of the journey passed quickly. Too soon, we pulled up outside the nondescript office building I'd visited almost two weeks earlier. I glanced up at its windows and grimaced in anticipation of the ordeal to come.

In the reception area, I gave my name and took a seat, welcoming the opportunity to get a better feel for the working environment. The décor was lacklustre: magnolia walls, relieved by occasional panels of maroon to match the newish-looking carpet tiles. But there were one or two decent paintings in the same style as the watercolour I'd noticed on my previous visit; and some large black-and-white blow-ups also caught my interest, various metal shapes whose purpose baffled me.

Phones rang, people came and went: the postman, visitors like myself, even a group of sixth-formers. The receptionists, often considered to be the barometer of an organisation, both seemed efficient and courteous — as well as being young and pretty.

At five past nine, the redhead came over to me with an apologetic smile. 'Jack's very sorry, but he'll be delayed about ten minutes. Would you like a cup of coffee?'

As her boss was paying handsomely for keeping me waiting, I smiled back. 'Thank you — white, no sugar.'

Ten minutes turned into twenty; I'd finished my coffee, read the front page of several issues of *Metal Matters* and lost some of my equilibrium. I picked up my bag and went over to the reception desk.

'I'd like to speak to Jack Smith's PA,'

I said to the redhead, as pleasantly as I could.

'Sure.' She dialled an extension, waited for several seconds, then replaced the receiver. 'No answer, Betsy must have just popped out for a minute — '

'Don't worry, I know my way.'

Before she could stop me, I made for the staircase — a monstrous feat of engineering, all shining brass handrails and balusters with the inevitable rampant lions as corner supports — and walked briskly to the first floor. Last time I'd taken the second door on the left, straight into the Chief Executive's office; this time I turned in at the first door, which was slightly ajar and bore the nameplate 'Betsy Walker'.

The room was empty, but the adjoining one was not. A familiar voice spilled through the open connecting door, the tone harsher than I'd ever heard it; someone had clearly rubbed the black velvet the wrong way this morning.

' . . . Not on my watch. The safety of the men on the shop floor comes first

— I don't give a toss about anything else!' A pause. 'And you'd better behave yourself tomorrow. We'll have a visitor, female, so watch your language.'

'What's a woman doing at a Leo Components union meeting?' Another man's voice; gruffer, with a thicker accent.

'She's giving me some coaching.'

A knowing guffaw. 'Coaching? What sport's that in — bedroom gymnastics?'

'Sod off, she's not my type. And even if she was, she'd freeze my bloody bollocks off at forty paces.'

'Not like the bird you were with at Zorro's the other week, eh? Saw it in the paper. Did she have anything on under that — ' Thanks to his accent, the rest was unintelligible.

And then they laughed, in that stupid nudge-nudge wink-wink way that men do — while I just stood there, overcome with anger and embarrassment. Which meant that, when they came through the door a few seconds later, my face drew their attention like a beacon.

I fixed Jack Smith with a look that would have made freezing his bollocks off seem like a merciful release. *So I'm not your type, am I? Funny, I got quite the opposite impression at our first meeting. Or are you just narked that I didn't instantly drop to my knees and worship the babe magnet of the North West?*

When he saw me he stopped dead, laughter fading to an uncertain smile. But I'd underestimated his powers of recovery. In two strides he was in front of me and somehow my hand was in his possession.

'Hi there, sorry to keep you waiting,' he said, tone softer now, eyes boring into mine. I deliberately flicked my gaze to the sturdy, balding man beside him who acknowledged me with a cautious nod. As if in retaliation, the grip on my fingers tightened. 'Let me introduce Nick Suggett, our union rep. Nick, this is Alicia Marlowe, my — er — coach.'

An awkward little silence; after a few seconds, I yanked my hand from his grasp and offered it to Nick Suggett with a polished smile. 'Pleased to meet you. And don't worry, you won't get frost-bite — I save that for my most troublesome clients.'

Nick's eyes crinkled as he shook my hand. 'Pleased to meet you, too. Good to hear you're keeping Jack under control.' An appraising look at both of us from under bushy brows. 'I'll leave you to your coaching, then.'

While he shuffled out of the room, I swept past Jack Smith into the adjoining office and settled myself in one of the black leather chairs. As before, I took out my laptop and opened a file labelled with his name. As before, I made myself look busy — this time, not so much to avoid conversation as to regain my composure.

'Coffee?' His voice, behind me.

'No, thank you. I had one while I was sitting in reception for twenty-five minutes.'

He prowled into my line of sight, hands in pockets, head down — a master class in mock humility. 'I've said I'm sorry. Something cropped up on the shop floor, and Nick wanted to speak to me urgently. That's what running this business is like.' A pause. 'Look, when I told him you weren't my type, that was — '

'Entirely mutual.' To drive the point home, I looked up at him, my face devoid of expression. 'In case you need a translation, that means you're not my type either. Which leads us seamlessly into your personality type and the questionnaire results. If you sit down, we can do an initial run-through before the management meeting.'

He hesitated, as if debating whether to obey. When at last he took the seat opposite me, I thrust a copy of the results at him. In my desperation to avoid physical contact, I let go too soon and the print-out slapped onto the glass-topped table. Unthinking, I reached over to pick it up — and our fingers snagged. I recoiled — a response so sudden and intense that I couldn't have covered it up, even if I'd wanted to.

He shot me a curious glance while he scooped up the papers. 'Is my personality that toxic?'

'Let's find out.' To my horror, my voice was little more than a croak. I cleared my throat — twice, for God's sake! — turned over the header page and succeeded in delivering my usual introduction about the value of self-awareness. 'We'll start by looking at whether you tend to be inwardly or outwardly focused. You are definitely the latter — read the description and see if it rings true.'

For a few moments there was silence; then he said, 'I suppose it does. 'You like to be in a fast-paced environment' — yes. 'You tend to work out ideas with others' — yes. 'Talkative' — yes. Although not so much when I'm with you.'

I ignored the last comment. 'Next we'll look at how you like to take in information. You'll see that you value concrete facts and details, and practical applications — more what we call 'sensing' than 'intuitive'.'

He studied the page and frowned. 'I think I'm both. Yes, when it comes to business targets I like to deal in specifics. But when it comes to people, my hunches tend to be right . . . I mean, as soon as I saw Nick this morning I knew he'd try to screw me over, and then I could tell that you — '

'What you could tell about me is irrelevant, we're confining our conversation to your working environment.' A slow, deep breath. 'Anyway, this is about preferences — it doesn't mean you're *not* intuitive. The third section shows how you make decisions. You're 'thinking' rather than 'feeling' — for example, you prefer to be fair at the expense of keeping people happy.'

'It also says I enjoy finding the flaws in an argument. So here's one — shouldn't you be asking the management team these questions instead of me? For all you know, I could be pulling the wool over your eyes and simply making up the answers.'

I smiled in spite of myself, relishing a challenge that I could meet head on. 'First, these questionnaires are designed to make that difficult to do and straightforward to detect. Second, since individual growth starts with *self*-awareness, you'd be doing yourself no favours. And third, as you've suggested, I will be gaining a more holistic and objective view of you through your interaction with others over the next few days.' I couldn't resist sowing the seeds of a future business opportunity, even though I wouldn't be involved. 'Sometimes we're asked to coach an entire Board, in which eventuality everyone completes the questionnaires — to inform both individual and team development.'

He stared back at me, as if pondering an intelligent reply; then he let out a low whistle and said, 'Have you been trained to talk like that, or does it come naturally?'

Once again I ignored the personal observation, took another deep breath and turned to the next page. 'The final section describes the framework for your outer life. You are clearly 'perceiving' more than 'judging'. As you can see, this means a flexible approach to rules and deadlines, a preference for improvisation over planning — which can be a source of employee conflict, underperformance and frustration.'

For once his smile didn't reach his eyes. 'Makes you wonder why anyone would want to work for such an arsehole, doesn't it? That reminds me, it's nearly time for the management meeting.'

I glanced at my watch in surprise: six minutes to ten. I'd been too busy concentrating on the conversational thrust and parry to notice. 'Wait, who's going to be at this meeting? I need an organisation chart, and — '

'Sorry, can't do that now — you'll just have to go with the flow. Talking of which, I'm off to the Gents.' He sprang to his feet, headed in the direction of his PA's room and poked his head round her door. ‘Betsy, show Alicia to the Boardroom, would you?’ A nod back at me, with a casual, ‘See you there in five.’

5

As senior management meetings went, I'd seen worse. But I'd also seen a lot better. My notes could have provided a case study in dictatorial leadership.

For a start, the content bore little resemblance to the official agenda; Jack Smith seemed to think that being chair allowed him to pursue one of his own. Even worse, his dominant style made sure that all communication was channelled through him — a breeding ground for cliques and corridor conversations outside the meeting.

When he introduced me as his executive coach, interest rippled round the table. To my relief, it was short-lived; once the meeting got under way, the other directors soon forgot I was there and I could observe their dysfunctional team behaviours more freely.

The only other woman in the room

was Betsy, who took the minutes and made valiant attempts at keeping the meeting on track. This was the homely PA I'd noted on my previous visit, and I watched closely how she and her boss interacted. No sign of any innuendo-filled banter from him, and she was more like a mother hen trying to control her large and demanding chick.

Needless to say, the meeting lasted far too long. Even the lunch did little to revive the flagging energy levels, consisting as it did of stilted informality and two courses of local stodge. I toyed with the steak and potato pie, and refused outright the jam roly-poly pudding. By four o'clock, everyone except Jack Smith seemed exhausted.

I waited until we were back in his office before I spoke to him. 'When would you like to discuss my observations on the meeting?'

He beamed at me. 'Went well, didn't it?'

Had we been in the same room? 'What specifically do you think went well?' I said, squeezing some neutrality into my voice.

Not enough, apparently, because his smile faltered. 'We got through the agenda, didn't we?'

'You got through *an* agenda, but I would dispute whether it was the one everyone had in front of them. Would you like to discuss this now?'

The merest hesitation; then, 'Sorry, I've got to catch up on some paperwork with Betsy. We can have a review over dinner.'

It wasn't a question, more a statement — an assumption, even — and I felt my face stiffen. 'I don't usually — '

'Oh well, it's up to you,' he put in, with a shrug. 'We can always stay here. There'll be no one to disturb us, I'm usually the last one to leave the office.'

I gave in to a little sigh of frustration. We definitely needed the review today, while it was all still fresh. Which left me two options to consider: being on my own with him here, or having dinner with him in a public place. With anyone else, I'd have simply stayed where I was and finished the day's work; but somehow with him that presented a bigger challenge . . .

'We've both got to eat sometime,' I said abruptly, 'so I suppose I'll have to say yes to dinner.'

He burst out laughing. 'Such enthusiasm! I've a good mind to whisk you off to the local greasy spoon for Grimshaw's best tripe and onions.'

'You can take me where you like, I don't have to eat the food.'

'Don't be daft — if you're not going to eat, we may as well stay here. Anyway, you need a decent meal — you hardly ate a thing earlier.'

'Ah yes, lunch.' I grimaced. 'Or should I say death by carbohydrate.'

'Never did me any harm.'

That was debatable, but I refrained from saying so.

I spent the next two and a half hours in Betsy's room, typing up a more detailed note of my observations and checking my emails. From time to time I broke off and listened to the voices next door, Jack's bass tones alternating with Betsy's quiet murmur. I'd met her type so often — the ideal PA, smoothing the wrinkles out of her boss's day before he even noticed them. I suspected, however, that her magic powers didn't extend to his personal life.

And then the voices stopped altogether. Betsy came back to tidy her desk, and we exchanged goodnights. I'd just packed away my laptop when he sauntered into the room in his shirt sleeves, jacket hooked over one shoulder, smile full on.

'Ready to go? We'll take my car — unless you want to follow in yours?'

'Not really, mine's two hundred miles away.'

'How did you get up here, then?'

'Let me see . . . My broomstick's having its MOT, so I must have got the train, mustn't I?'

A laugh, low and long. 'Careful, that sense of humour's showing again. Okay, I'll run you to your hotel afterwards.'

'No need, I'll get a taxi.'

'Give me a break, Alicia.'

In reply, I picked up my bag and made for the door. Whether his words were a meaningless aside or a serious request, it was best to leave well alone.

We went down the monstrous staircase and out into the sticky evening air. I'd have picked out his big flashy car instantly, even if it hadn't been parked in the chief executive's designated space. He opened the passenger door and held out his hand for my bag. I gave him my jacket, too — but felt no cooler in my long-sleeved, high-necked shirt. I almost suggested we went back to my hotel so that I could change — except that he might take that as blatant encouragement. I fastened my belt, settled back into the leather seat — and found that it reclined a little too much for my liking. I searched quickly for a lever to adjust it.

'Need some help?' The black velvet was back, and threaded with amusement. 'Which way do you want me to adjust it?'

'Upright, of course,' I said edgily, banishing any thoughts of the alternative. As a further precaution, I slanted my legs away from him — just in case he had to reach over and fumble under my seat. But it was all done with the press of a button.

Once he'd accelerated away from Leo Components, he loosened his tie and turned up the air conditioning. 'Not too breezy?'

'No, it's fine.' We left the industrial estate behind and took an unfamiliar route among terraces of red-brick houses, their scraps of garden struggling into summer bloom. 'Where are we going?'

'The best Italian this side of Manchester.' He glanced across at me. 'Do you like pasta? I meant to check.'

'That's fine,' I said, wondering what constituted a good Italian restaurant in Grimshaw. And when we drew up outside an unassuming little place in the middle of a row of shops, it looked as though my worst fears were realised. Especially since its name, Corleone's, rang a bell — and not just because I'd sat through three *Godfather* films. I recalled something from my research, an incident involving Jack Smith, a model called Tracey Turnbull and Tracey's ex, a Manchester United player. The ex had eventually been escorted off the premises; shortly afterwards Jack had left with Tracey — and a black eye.

Once we were inside, however, I couldn't help warming to the place: cream walls, dark wooden floor and furniture — a sort of rustic chic. We were greeted cordially by the manager and shown to a large alcove, with some mumbling about 'Signor Jack's usual table'. Surprise, surprise. Here the lighting was more subdued, the ambience more intimate: a scene set for seduction.

As we sat down, I saw that we were lucky to get in; the restaurant was packed. A thought crossed my mind, and my lips tightened. 'Had you already booked this table for tonight?'

He pretended to study the wine list. 'Do you prefer red or white? I can recommend — '

'I prefer you to be straight with me.'

That made him look up. 'Do you? I wonder.'

I narrowed my eyes. 'Which means?'

'Which means yes, I booked the table last week.'

That wasn't what my second question referred to, but I let it pass. 'So this was all planned?'

'Not exactly, more on the off chance.' He bent his head over the wine list again. 'Do you fancy sharing a bottle of Chianti?'

The off chance — of what? That dinner in his usual restaurant at his usual table would result in the usual outcome?

'No, thank you,' I said coldly.

'Don't you drink alcohol?'

'Not while I'm working.'

'Fair enough.'

We ordered drinks: a beer for him, a lime and soda for me. The waiter greeted him like an old friend, and me with undisguised curiosity. To show that this was a business meeting and nothing more, I took out my notebook and placed it on the table in a prominent position.

We reviewed our menus in silence. When the waiter returned, I looked up — and found Jack staring at me.

A shiver coursed through me. This was just like the first dinner with Troy, long ago in LA. Oh, not in every detail — for a start, the restaurant had been Peruvian, not Italian — but the eyes holding mine in the candlelight were equally magnetic, the scrutiny of a stranger equally unnerving. Or perhaps, as then, it was more a feeling of intoxication . . .

'Everything okay? You look as though you've seen a ghost.' Jack's voice was soft, almost tender.

I shrank back in my chair, and shut the menu with a snap. 'I'll have the rigatoni, with a side salad.'

The waiter nodded. 'Thank you,

Signorina. And for you, Signor Jack?'

'The usual, please, Luigi.'

As soon as we were on our own again, he said, 'Did you?'

'Did I what?'

'See a ghost.'

'There's no point in asking me anything personal, because I won't give you an answer. It's one of my ground rules for coaching. Speaking of which,' — I opened my notebook — 'I've made a list of what we need to discuss.'

'Don't, Alicia, not yet. Let's chill out for a moment.'

My lip curled. 'Chill out? Isn't there a risk that I might freeze off certain parts of your anatomy, as you so delicately put it to Nick Suggett this morning?'

His sudden laugh made heads turn. 'Just when I think you're a lost cause, you come out with something that creases me up.'

'What do you mean — a lost cause?'

He hesitated, as if choosing his words. 'You're all about work, it's as though you can't interact with people — with me — on any other level. Don't take this the wrong way, but — '

I cut in with, 'Which other way would you like me to take it?'

'Look, I work hard too — but at least I know how to relax.'

'And I don't?'

'Not that I've noticed. I've never met a woman like you before, so . . . ' — he lowered his gaze and traced the tablecloth with his forefinger — ' . . . joyless.'

I flinched, but recovered myself instantly. 'And what's your definition of joy? Getting laid every five minutes?'

The tracing stopped. 'Why would you think that?' he said, not looking up.

'Oh, come on! In the past month alone you've had Lisa, followed by Tracey — although she didn't last long after that little incident in this very restaurant, did she? Then at least six more whose names I can't remember. And they're only the ones that get press coverage, goodness knows how many others you've slept with.'

For the first time, I saw him redden; and he still didn't look at me. 'You've done your homework all right. How far back did you go?'

'Three or four months. That was enough, it told me all I needed to know.'

He drained his glass and gestured to the waiter; then turned to me, his face hard and set. 'Why've you been digging around my private life? You've just told me that yours is off limits, so why isn't mine?'

I unfolded the cream napkin and spread it over my lap. It was starched, unyielding, the epitome of joylessness . . . I forced myself to make eye contact with him. 'I only researched what was publicly and readily available. As there was hardly any information about you or your company in my normal sources, I simply widened the net a little. The relevance of your extracurricular activities is obvious, they give me an insight into your values. If you mess around in your personal life, the chances are you'll do the same in business.'

Now it was his turn to flinch, just as the waiter returned. 'Signor Jack?'

'A bottle of sparkling water, Luigi. To go with the conversation.' He looked across at me; this time, his expression was blank.

'And another thing,' I said, dismissing any qualms about broaching a potentially sensitive subject in a busy restaurant, 'why is the fact that today should have been your father's retirement date so significant? Because you were obviously stressed out when you realised you couldn't reschedule the senior management meeting.'

He shifted in his chair. 'Have you seen any particular signs of stress today?'

'Not really — '

'Then forget it.' His eyes held mine in a mute appeal for co-operation. 'Please.'

We lapsed into an uncomfortable silence until Luigi brought the water.

When we were on our own again, I opened my notebook and said briskly,

'Shall we go through my list?' He nodded, still without speaking.

Such a relief to focus on business; I outlined my observations as succinctly as possible and finished by asking for his comments. Before he could reply, however, our meal arrived. I decided to continue the feedback session tomorrow; he'd probably had enough self-awareness for one day.

The rigatoni primavera looked and smelled inviting. I tasted one mouthful and discovered I was ravenous. Jack's 'usual' turned out to be a hefty steak, with parmesan-sprinkled spaghetti and salad. He pushed it around his plate, then said, 'I didn't realise I was doing such a crap job. Looks like it'll take longer than six months to get me sorted.'

'You'd be surprised at what coaching can achieve in that time.' A pang — professional pride, or guilt? — as I remembered that I wouldn't be around to see the results. 'This is delicious, by the way. How's your steak?'

'I'm not hungry.' He put down his knife and fork. Sensing danger, I fixed my gaze on my food and braced myself. He said, 'At our first meeting, you talked about the need for trust between us during the coaching. So why don't you trust me?'

A sip of lime and soda. 'What makes you think — '

'You won't even let me drive you back to your hotel.'

'It's out of your way — '

'How do you know?'

'I don't, but it's a good ten miles from Grimshaw.'

'That's not a problem.' A short pause. 'Will you let me give you a lift?'

Our eyes met; and, once again, his suggested a different, deeper, question than the spoken one. 'To prove to both of us that you trust me,' he added, quietly.

If only it was that simple . . . But I'd got this far unscathed; why not let him drive me back to High Stone Hall? 'Yes,' I said, with a smile. And, for the first time, I let the smile reach my eyes. As though, despite my lingering reservations, I needed to show him that I felt at ease in his company.

'Wow,' he said.

'I agree, this *is* something of a breakthrough in our coaching relationship.'

'Actually, I was thinking what a great smile you have.'

I blushed, disposed of the smile and took refuge in my rigatoni, irritated that I'd given him any encouragement. But after that his appetite improved, and he finished his meal before I did. Over coffee, we traded careful small talk about Italy. We'd visited the same part of Milan, and spent time in the same gallery between business meetings. I congratulated myself on my handling of this shared interest in art; it had evolved from silent disbelief to almost animated discussion.

And then it all went pear-shaped.

I saw her before he did. A deceptively dishevelled blonde mane, perfect make-up, dazzling jewellery and plunging neckline — making her determined way to our table.

He looked up just as she shimmied to a halt beside him.

'Well, Jack, fancy seeing you here.' Her speech was unexpectedly cultured, and slightly slurred.

'Karina.'

I couldn't read the expression on his face, but I could hear his intake of breath after speaking her name. And I saw how he closed his eyes when she bent to brand the corner of his mouth with her lips.

Then she straightened up and glanced haughtily in my direction — just long enough, it seemed, to discard me as competition. Resentment surged through me; it wasn't often that I felt under-dressed and overawed.

'Naughty me,' she drawled, 'I didn't realise you had company.'

Like hell; she'd have spotted me from the other side of the restaurant and, I suspected, staged her little show of playful intimacy purely for my benefit.

Was it even authentic? I couldn't recall reading about anyone by the name of Karina, but perhaps she pre-dated my research.

'Jack.' Her tone sharpened. 'Aren't you going to introduce me?'

His eyes flickered open. 'Leave it, Karina — '

I held out my hand. 'Alicia Marlowe.'

Her fingers skimmed mine. 'You're not from round here?' Then, as she spotted my notebook, 'Are you a reporter?'

My most brilliant smile. 'More of a behavioural psychologist.' I couldn't resist adding, 'But I'm not working tonight.' Luckily for her — because I could have filled half the notebook with my observations on her antics so far. I finished with a husky, 'Jack and I are enjoying getting to know each other.'

I looked across the table to assess the impact of those last few words. Surely he would take them in the right spirit, nothing more? A united front against the woman who'd disturbed our dinner

— in very different ways, it seemed.

I needn't have worried; it was as if he hadn't even heard me. He said, 'Is Henrik here?'

She gave a fragile laugh. 'He was, but we had a row and he left in a bit of a hurry. Was that before we saw you, or after? Can't remember. Anyway, he ordered me a taxi — it's here now, but . . . ' Her voice trailed off and she swayed prettily towards him, as if the very thought of using hired transport had sapped her energy.

He jumped to his feet and caught her in his arms. 'I'll drive you home.' His eyes met mine over the top of her golden head, their expression unfathomable. 'Alicia, why don't you take the taxi that's outside? I'll pay for the meal.'

'I'd rather pay my half — '

'Forget it.' A pause. 'Especially since this evening didn't work out as planned.' Although I knew he was talking about finishing the feedback session, I wondered if he wanted to give Karina a different impression. Maybe a bit of sexual rivalry turned them both on — and of course I'd added to the intrigue by positioning our dinner as 'enjoying getting to know each other'. Now I wished I hadn't, if only to rid myself of this feeling — however ridiculous — that I'd lost out to *her*. Because there was no doubt in my mind that they'd be spending the night together, Henrik or no Henrik.

Back in my hotel room, I managed to refrain from surfing the net for references to Jack and Karina. After all, he meant nothing to me, absolutely nothing.

But the word 'joyless' hounded my thoughts, until at last I fell into an exhausted sleep.

6

Next morning I returned to Leo Components weighed down with baggage: laptop, suitcase and the remains of a throbbing headache. Up in his office, it looked as if Jack too had barely slept — no doubt for an entirely different reason. The angles of his face seemed more pronounced, casting shadows where yesterday there were none; his hair was sticking up at the front as if someone had just run their fingers through it.

I averted my eyes before he caught me staring.

The first thing he said was, 'Sorry about last night, I didn't expect to have to rush off like that.'

For some reason this rankled. 'You seem to be making a habit of apologising after every meeting we have. Perhaps you need to change your underlying behaviour.'

A weary smile. 'Something else for me to work on.'

'And I can't believe you didn't *expect* what happened. If you choose to eat at a popular restaurant in your local town, isn't it likely that you'll bump into someone you know? Although I must admit the speed with which you left wasn't exactly flattering.'

He reddened. 'I've said I'm sorry. Now, if you don't mind, I need to prepare for the union meeting.'

'So do I.' I spun on my heel and stormed into Betsy's room.

In her calming presence, I recovered my composure and asked for the meeting agenda and attendee list. A mix of Leo Components and Sphinx Industries representatives, with Jack chairing, Betsy taking minutes and the HR Director, Phil, no doubt there to defend his territory. The same group had probably already met during the acquisition negotiations, but that was history. I knew that, as the UK manufacturing industry was still heavily unionised, the newly formed company would succeed or fail based on the discussions round this table. Jack's dictatorial style would be highly counter-productive, and I couldn't help feeling nervous on his behalf.

I needn't have worried. It looked like he'd taken all my feedback on board and — even more remarkable — worked out how to act on it. He started with introductions, triggering the inevitable amusement when he described me as his executive coach, and then embarked on the next agenda item — 'Vision'. Instead of pitching his own thoughts, however, he asked each of the attendees to outline three wishes for the company.

It was a shrewd move. He effectively handed the floor to the union representatives, but forced them to put aside any confrontational speeches they might have prepared in favour of constructive ideas. Accordingly, when conflict emerged, it was among themselves — and not directed at him, their original target. As they spoke, he captured the main themes on a flip chart. Betsy kept glancing meaningfully at her watch, but he ignored her.

Only when the heated discussion had run its natural course did he sit down at the table again. 'Excellent, we have the makings of a great vision for our new company. If I can summarise, starting with where we are now . . . Phil, you pointed out that we've got a North-South divide: a sharp decline in the manufacturing power base of the North, and the growing dominance of London as a global financial centre. But we agreed that we can't afford to dwell on this, that our company needs to change — unless we want to see more local communities destroyed. And you've given me a clear picture of what change looks like' — he gestured to the flip-chart — 'with some common themes coming through. Like transforming our approach to employee relations, such as self-managed teams and profit sharing. And that suggestion of yours, Nick, about making manufacturing sexy again — that's why we've been arranging visits for local schools, but there's a lot more we can do with our apprenticeship schemes.' He paused and looked briefly at each of us in turn. 'I haven't felt so positive about the future in a long time. Nothing we've talked about here is impossible, but we need to turn words into action. That'll mean additional investment in areas which we've traditionally neglected. Can I rely on your support if I put a business case to the Board?'

Heads nodded round the table; then, to Betsy's obvious relief, we moved more quickly through the rest of the agenda. There were still points of contention, but Jack had removed the sting. The meeting ended with a sandwich lunch which, by yesterday's standards, was light and healthy. As we ate, we split into various conversational groups: Nick talking about the football transfer window with two of the Sphinx men; Jack and the remaining union representatives, too far away for me to overhear; Phil, Betsy and I comparing notes on holidays in Spain.

When Phil left the table to go to another meeting, Jack came to sit in his place beside me. 'I thought we'd leave for the Lakes mid-afternoon, once I've finished off a few things with Betsy. Is that okay?'

'Of course. We can discuss this meeting when we're in the car — or tonight, after dinner.'

He laughed. 'Believe me, after one of Mitch's meals you won't be in a fit state to do anything except sleep. Anyway, I wouldn't want to get indigestion.'

'From all those unpalatable truths?' I smiled. 'Perhaps there aren't quite as many as last time.'

'I hope not. After yesterday's meeting I downloaded some management books and stayed up all bloody night reading two of them.'

My smile faded. He must be lying; he would hardly have spent the night in bed with Karina *reading*. I pushed my plate away, unable to finish my second sandwich.

'Something wrong?' he said, frowning.

'No, I've just had enough. Excuse me.' I scrambled to my feet, left the room and took refuge in the Ladies. At least he couldn't follow me in there.

When I came out, Nick was waiting. 'Jack asked me to show you the factory.' He looked me up and down. 'We'll stick to the viewing gallery, less of a distraction for the lads. No offence, but on Friday afternoons concentration's not at its best.'

Strange, wasn't it? From someone like Nick Suggett, this behaviour seemed nothing more than quaintly sexist and rather pathetic. Whereas the same looks and words from his boss would have produced a very different reaction . . .

I said abruptly, 'Aren't there *any* women working on the factory floor? These days jobs have to be open to both genders, you can't discriminate.'

He shrugged. 'The women prefer office jobs, always have. But Jack's trying to get the local sixth-formers interested in apprenticeships, girls as well as boys. Can't see it working myself, but good on him for trying. Anyway, come and see the Leo Components production line.'

I followed him down the back staircase — far less impressive than the front one — then out into an enclosed yard, bleak as a prison. I could hear a strange muffled clanking, although there wasn't an obvious source. As we approached a tall brick building opposite, the noise got louder. When Nick opened a huge metal door and ushered me inside, I almost reeled. A row of machines confronted me, each as big as a room, pounding and hissing in a relentless rhythm. And the heat . . . unbearable.

To my relief, we escaped up a flight of steps and into a room with thirty-odd chairs facing a large wall-mounted TV screen. Cooler and much, much quieter. The wall behind the chairs was a sheet of glass, overlooking the factory floor.

'Take a seat.' Nick busied himself with a laptop, while I settled myself in the back row. I found that the chair swivelled, so that I could watch either the screen or the factory. I smiled at the thought of a bunch of teenagers let loose in here, endlessly spinning — to the despair of their teachers.

A cough from Nick drew my attention. 'There's a company video here which explains what we do, then I'll show you the different processes through the window.'

I hadn't the heart to say that I'd already watched a similar video on the company website. In any case, he talked over it — mainly about Jack. It seemed that his appointment as Chief Exec had marked a turning point in the company's fortunes. Investment for the latest technology in deep draw stamping? Jack had got the Board's seal of approval. More aggressive management of key customer accounts? Jack had masterminded the plan and secured the funding to implement it. Better community relations? Jack had offered the old company football field to the local youth teams and was now raising money for its maintenance and improvement.

'Makes you wonder why he needs a coach,' I said drily, when I could get a word in.

'Oh, don't get me wrong — he's got plenty of faults. And some of the managers resent him like hell. But he's given the lads here hope, and that's an achievement in itself. You see, Jack started on the factory floor too — ' He looked over my shoulder. 'Shit! Looks like Maggie's in trouble, I'd better go down there and sort her out.' And he dashed out of the viewing gallery before I could ask him who he was talking about.

I turned to scan the factory floor, but I couldn't see anyone remotely like a Maggie. Anyway, hadn't Nick just told me that all the female employees were office workers? And then Jack strode into view, loosening his tie and collar, rolling up his sleeves, listening intently to a smaller man at his side who was half-running to keep up. When they stopped at one of the machines, Nick joined them and they stood for a while, deep in a discussion punctuated by occasional gestures at various dials and displays. Finally Jack reached up and wrenched a lever, bracing his body to increase the force. I stared down at him, absorbing every detail.

What was it he'd said earlier about making manufacturing sexy? Take a well-built man, shirt half off, applying himself to a physical task with power and purpose . . . Job done.

He glanced up, caught me looking at him and grinned; I blushed like a teenager and swivelled my chair away from the window. When the viewing gallery door opened a few minutes later, my gaze was fixed on the TV screen — although I had no idea what I was watching.

'Sorry, Alicia.' Nick's voice, slightly out of breath. 'Maggie's a bit temperamental — '

'Who *is* Maggie? I didn't see her — '

He chuckled. 'Yes, you did — she's

our new sixty-three-tonne power press. No one can pronounce the name of the company who built her, so we call her Maggie for short. She cost God knows how much, produces components twice as fast as the old one and I've already suggested to Jack that he moves in with her. Can't keep his hands off her, I think he's programmed her to go wrong deliberately.'

I risked a look back through the window, but Jack had gone. His performance today intrigued me: one minute eloquent and visionary at the union meeting, the next hands on and practical in the factory. It made me wonder which man I'd be spending the weekend with . . .

The video rolled on, and Nick continued his voiceover. There were no more insights into Jack Smith, however, and I found it difficult to concentrate on the technical detail. As soon as we reached the end, I thanked him for his time and asked him to show me the way back to Jack's office. I felt exhausted, and anxious to get the journey to the Lakes under way; if there were any unpleasant surprises in store, I wanted them over and done with.

But Jack's office was empty. Swallowing my disappointment, I retrieved my laptop from my bag and sat down, intending to distract myself with my emails.

The interconnecting door with Betsy's room was, as usual, slightly ajar, and I could hear her taking a succession of phone calls. For each one, she went through the same routine: no, Jack wasn't available; yes, she would pass on the message. As her tone grew noticeably less patient, it dawned on me that all these calls must be from the same person.

And then I heard *his* voice, asking if something or other was ready, and Betsy saying, 'Fat chance, what with the phone going non-stop all afternoon. I gave up on writing down all the messages — basically, Karina wants you to call her.'

Emails forgotten, scruples ignored, I

leaned towards the door so that I didn't miss a single word.

'Did she say why?' He sounded wary — or maybe cautiously optimistic?

'Just that it's urgent. But then it always was with her, wasn't it?' A pause. 'Jack, I'm worried. I don't understand why she's calling you at the office, out of the blue.'

Her concern was palpable. I noted the shift in her manner, from work-based camaraderie to a display of personal loyalty, however understated. For some reason, I thought of Nick's words earlier — 'he's given the lads here hope'. And I realised that Jack Smith had deeper qualities than I'd originally thought.

Next door there was silence for a moment; then he said quietly, 'Because she can't get me on my mobile. I changed my number, remember?'

'No, I mean why's she calling you *now*? It's been over for a good six months, and you were so sure your 'Karina campaign' was working.'

He cleared his throat. 'We saw her last night, at Corleone's. She was in a bit of a state, I had to take her home.'

'Oh, *Jack*.'

'What else could I do?'

'I know.' A loud sigh. 'You'd better ring her back, then — hadn't you? I expect you won't want to use your mobile. You can call her on my office phone while I pop along to Accounts and get those reports you're after.'

Was that just a ruse to give him some privacy? Maybe I should have done the same and brought my eavesdropping to an end; but I couldn't tear myself away.

Another silence; then I heard him say, 'Hi, it's me.' An economy of words that spoke volumes; I found myself closing my eyes, as if to shut out their intimacy. He continued, 'Feeling better? . . . That's good . . . Yes, it was . . . No, it didn't matter at all . . . I know, but . . . Well, if that's what you want . . . Tell him, then . . . I can't, I'm away for the weekend . . . Yes, staying with Bill and Mitch . . . You never did, did you?

. . . No, Karina, that's not a good idea.'

It was easy to imagine the other side of the conversation and fill in the gaps: she would be seeking reassurance about last night, suggesting that she dispensed with Henrik, asking to see Jack again this evening. What a shame — for both of them — that he'd made other plans. I smiled grimly to myself; he obviously couldn't bring himself to mention that his plans included me.

Then it seemed that one of them — I'd have loved to know who — hung up on the other. My eyes fluttered open, and I made a determined effort to appear engrossed in my inbox.

Jack breezed into the room a few seconds later. 'Right, time to set off.' His tone was light and cheerful, as if nothing had happened. 'I told Bill we'd get to Threlkeld by six o'clock — let's hope we have a clear run.' In a show of reluctance I kept my eyes fixed on my laptop screen for a little longer, before slowly lifting my gaze. With a flicker of surprise, instantly masked, I found him standing too close. He was dressed differently, more casually than before, an open-necked shirt and chinos. There was something about him — a freshness, maybe — that made me feel too hot, too formal.

'Should I change my clothes too?' I asked, hesitantly.

'Good idea. We don't want poor Bill thinking he's getting a last-minute VAT inspection.' He switched on that disarming grin and, despite the slur on my business suit, I found I couldn't rise to the bait. Maybe I was simply too tired to care.

'Give me ten minutes.'

It took less than that to wheel my suitcase to the Ladies, wash my face and slip on jeans, T-shirt and trainers. I kept a sweater with me as well, in case the weather turned cooler in the hills. But a glance in the mirror stopped me in my tracks: my French pleat now looked ridiculously out of place. I quickly undid it and let my hair swing loose around my shoulders.

When I returned to his office, his eyes widened — although all he said was 'okay, let's go' as he picked up my case. On the way out, I fully expected to run a gauntlet of stares and nudges — but I noticed none; perhaps he left early every Friday with a woman and a suitcase in tow.

We reached his car. While he put the cases in the boot, I opened the passenger door — and stopped dead. The seat was back in its semi-reclining position; hardly surprising, given the woman he'd taken home yesterday. No doubt they'd started in the car what they'd finished in the bedroom. I almost recoiled at the very thought of taking her place, but managed to pull myself together and get into the car.

This time, Jack needed no prompting to adjust my seat. And, as if he could read my mind, he stumbled through an explanation about needing to make Karina comfortable, because she kept falling asleep. Totally unconvincing.

We travelled the first few miles in

silence. This latest reminder of last night's humiliations, real or imagined, as well as the car's stop-start progression through a maze of road works, didn't encourage conversation — let alone a coaching debrief.

Once we joined the M6, however, the traffic flowed more freely and I regained my composure, launching into a comparison of today's meeting with yesterday's, from the perspective of his performance and learning. During the discussion that followed, I stared out of the passenger window to avoid looking at him. But that didn't fully protect me from his sense of humour; or charm, when he chose to use it.

As the business talk subsided, I started to feel uneasy — almost nauseous. Oh, he was a good driver; no problem there. This was more about me and my ripped-open wounds of recollection. *Those road trips with Troy, along the Pacific Coast Highway, up to Napa and Yosemite, down to Mexico . . . Except that, for much of the time, I hardly noticed the scenery — did I? Take a high-spec car, an unerring ability to find secluded parking areas, and lovers who couldn't keep their hands off each other . . . No wonder the trips became a succession of 'why wait?' moments.*

Oh yes, that faraway summer I'd learnt all about love, if that's what it was. And, when it was all over, I'd vowed that I'd never be played for such a fool again.

Jack made sporadic attempts at conversation. Each time, I blinked rapidly and struggled with a non-committal murmur in response, before retreating to the past. It was as if my finger was hovering over the self-destruct button.

And then came the hills, transforming the landscape from the ravages of industry to a gods' playground. Some spanned the horizon like the shoulders of giants; others flanked us so closely that I could almost have reached out and touched them. Lower, greener expanses were speckled with grazing sheep and stunted trees; higher up, waterfalls streaked white against bare rock. The broad ribbon of motorway twisted and turned between them, silvered by the sun; no sign of the famous rain.

Perhaps Jack sensed my brightening mood, because he broke the silence once more. 'Pennines on the right, Lakeland fells on the left. When I was young, I climbed most of them with the Venture Scouts. Kept me out of trouble, my mother always reckoned.' A pause. 'I was even angrier than most sixteen-year-olds, but that's another story.'

A sudden image came to mind, a scowling, lanky, black-haired boy in uniform; I managed a wan smile. 'Maybe you should take it up again.'

'Oh, I will — but it's not just about having the time, it's about having the right person to do it with.'

I tried to picture him and Karina hillwalking — and failed.

When at last we left the M6 behind, the contrast couldn't have been more marked. The roads were narrow, edged with dry-stone walls and crawling with traffic. Every so often a string of cottages on either side, with the occasional shop or pub, indicated a village: rural communities, presumably revitalised each spring by the tourist trade. I wondered if Threlkeld would be any different . . . Which reminded me — I needed to prepare for meeting our hosts.

'How have you positioned the purpose of this weekend with Bill and Mitch?' I said, briskly. With any other client, it was a question I would have asked much earlier; except, of course, with any other client I wouldn't have been in this situation.

A lengthy pause before he spoke. 'Let me give you the background. Bill's been a customer of Leo Components for over twenty years, but I only got to know him when I moved into sales — '

'I didn't realise you'd been in sales. I thought you'd always been in production.'

'It wasn't that big a jump, more a technical sales role. And I only did it for a couple of years, a stepping stone to general management. Anyway, as Bill's factory's near Glasgow, we used to meet half way — Penrith, just off the M6, north-eastern part of the Lake District. Then we started doing a spot of fishing together, and Mitch would come down and join us — '

'But I thought they lived here? Isn't Blencathra Lodge their home?'

'It's their holiday home. They bought it last year, for their silver wedding anniversary.'

I frowned. 'I thought same-sex marriages were only legalised recently.'

A puzzled glance across at me. 'What makes you think it's a same-sex marriage?'

'Isn't Mitch a he?'

He burst out laughing. '*Midge* is very definitely a she!'

'Midge? As in another name for a mosquito?'

'Bill says it applies just as much to

her, since she's small, annoying and frequently found in Scotland.'

'Mmm.' I was too busy working through this new information to share the joke. Did it matter that Midge was female? Probably not. But it mattered that I'd made assumptions instead of checking everything out. And all because, for the first time in a while, I'd let a man get to me . . .

Now he was asking me a question; I roused myself from the depths of self-reproach. 'Sorry?'

'I said, did you notice the painting in my office?'

'The watercolour?' I recalled the slate-grey lake, the snow-capped hills. 'Is it of somewhere in the Lake District?'

'Yes — Grasmere. We're near there now — keep looking out of your window, you'll soon see the lake. And Wordsworth's buried in the village churchyard — mind, he'd be hard pressed to 'wander lonely as a cloud' these days, wouldn't he, with all these people around?'

'You don't have to be alone to be lonely,' I said, half to myself.

A swift, appraising look. 'You're right, that was a stupid thing to say. Anyway, the painting's a Midge original.'

'Oh? I liked it.'

'I've got a few more of hers, in the reception area and at home.' And he went on to describe — at unnecessary length — her burgeoning career as a Lakeland artist, how she'd sparked an interest in art that he'd never had at school, his tentative attempts at painting in the privacy of her studio. Only half listening, I leaned back on the head rest, soothed by the gentle thrum of the car and the now-familiar timbre of his voice . . .

I awoke in a panic, my mind spinning with questions. How long had I been asleep? Where were we? And the most ridiculous thought of all — had I slept with my mouth open? A frantic sidelong glance at Jack left me none the wiser. As he turned his head, I looked hastily away — just in time to see the road sign. Only two miles to Threlkeld.

Two miles? We'll be there in five minutes, at most.

A surge of nausea. 'Look, I need to know — what *have* you told Bill and Midge about this weekend?'

He swung the car down a strip of tarmac, little more than a lane. 'That's what I've been trying to explain. Bill's more than a customer, he's a really good friend, and so's Midge.' He hesitated, as though uncertain of his ground — or my reaction. Somewhere in the back of my mind, an alarm bell jangled. He continued, 'They won't be in a hurry to talk to you about me unless they feel completely relaxed with both of us, with our . . . relationship, for want of a better word.'

A sharp left into a long driveway leading to a creeper-clad cottage. Pretty enough, but my immediate thought was — *that doesn't look big enough for three bedrooms!* In front of us, a tortoiseshell cat sprawling on the honey-gold gravel; beyond, with her back to us, a woman in bright blue trousers mowing a square of lawn. As we crunched across the gravel, the cat sprang up and scuttled behind an old stone trough crammed with trailing pink geraniums.

My hands clenched slowly in my lap. 'What exactly are you saying?'

The car eased to a halt and he switched off the ignition. Even so, I could barely hear the muffled drone of the lawn mower for the ringing in my ears; a simple sign of stress — or that imaginary alarm bell, now frighteningly real?

Our eyes met — mine hostile, his defensive. I watched dry-mouthed as he slid his gaze away, to the cottage, and the woman in the distance.

At last he owned up. 'I've sort of let them believe . . . Well, they think you're my new girlfriend.'

7

I stared at him in horror. 'They *what*?'

He turned back to me with an appraising look. 'I know, not an ideal situation. Let me explain.' His tone was calm, almost conversational. 'Whenever I've visited them here, in the last year or so — which hasn't been as often as I'd have liked, but still — I've always been on my own. So when I first mentioned bringing you . . . Well, before I knew what was happening, they'd made all sorts of assumptions — and I didn't have the heart to disappoint them.'

I let out a long, shuddering breath. 'You can't be serious.'

The ghost of a smile. 'We'll just have to make the best of it. You never know, it might even be fun.'

'I'm not here to have *fun*,' — I almost spat the word at him — 'I'm here to work.'

He raised an eyebrow. 'Can't you do both at the same time?'

Not any more. Not since I had 'fun' with my Californian coach. And even then, I took it all far more seriously than he did . . .

A shake of my head, an attempt to dismiss the tainted memories of one man and the disturbing revelations of the other. 'This is *exactly* the kind of compromising situation I warned you about, and I'll be taking the appropriate — '

'Look, as you've just said, you've got a job to do — we just need to play our parts well enough so that you can do it.' He added, almost casually, 'And anyway, it's only what you suggested last night, in the restaurant.'

This brought me up short. 'The restaurant?'

'Yes, when you made out to Karina that we were on a date.'

I felt the colour flood my face. 'That was different — '

'How?'

'It just *was*.'

An awkward pause, filled by the hum of the lawn mower. When it sputtered to a stop, all I could hear was the thump, thump, thump of my heart.

He glanced out of the window. 'She's seen us, we haven't got much time.' As if sensing my fear, he went on, 'I've already told you, you're safe with me. So really, this is the perfect solution. We'll put on a show for the McGraws, but whenever we're on our own it's back to normal.'

But what exactly was 'normal' between the two of us? Coaching him was becoming more and more like — like sinking into quicksand. 'I don't — ' I began, but my throat was too tight to go on.

'Alicia, trust me. It'll be okay.' He reached over and covered my hand with his. Lightly, no doubt to reassure. It did anything but.

I grabbed the door handle with my other hand — God knows why, there was nowhere to run. In any case, it was too late; the woman — Midge — was hurrying towards us. Jack released my hand and got out of the car, leaving me to deal with the lingering heat of his touch. I watched him scoop her into a bear hug, heard their laughter. From what I could see, she was indeed small, and fiftyish, with a nut-brown face and spiky fair hair. Nothing like Karina — which was something to be thankful for. But that didn't mean that I was ready to play along with Jack's idea of 'fun'.

Then he was opening my door, looking down at me with an expression that I couldn't read. 'Ready for this?' It was spoken softly, so that only I could hear.

With a deep, slightly ragged breath, I left the relative sanctuary of the car and offered Midge a tentative hand, which she ignored.

'Och, Alicia, don't be shy.' She embraced me warmly and kissed me on both cheeks. 'The way Jack talks about you, I feel as if we've known each other for years.'

What the hell had he said? More to the point — if there was a script, shouldn't he have shared it with me first? But I forced a smile and said politely, 'Lovely to meet you too.'

'Where's Bill?' Jack said.

'In the back garden with the barbecue, I've got Keswick Fire Brigade on standby.' An impish grin. 'First things first. Come with me, both of you — I need to show you something.'

'I'll get Alicia's case,' Jack said, while I followed Midge into the cottage and up a narrow staircase onto a landing. A tiny landing, with only two doors. The implications were obvious, and my stomach lurched.

'By the way, Midge,' — Jack's voice, behind me — 'I've got a bit of a cold coming on, so I told Alicia she could have the spare bedroom all to herself.' I felt my body relax; at least we wouldn't have to share anything other than a pretence. He went on, 'I'll make do with Hermann.'

I turned to him with a nervous laugh.

'Who's Hermann?'

'Our old motorhome,' Midge put in. 'A Hymer, so we had to go with something German.'

I stared at her blankly, while she went on, 'People with motorhomes like to give them names, and the names tend to reflect the nationality of the manufacturer.'

'And people with motorhomes are usually very fussy about who they allow to stay in them,' Jack said, grinning broadly. 'In fact, Midge and Bill have been known to let their guests stay in the house and move into Hermann themselves.'

She laughed. 'Nice try, but these days we prefer the comfort of our own bed. And I'm afraid it'll have to be Hermann for both of you — the spare bedroom's just not usable. See for yourselves.' She flung open the door on the right and led us into a completely empty room — no bed, no furniture of any kind, not even a carpet. I stared at the damp-ravaged ceiling and wall opposite, and tried to believe that this was just a very bad dream. A thud beside me — Jack, letting my suitcase drop to the floor-boards, as if equally aghast. Or was this a role play within a role play, and something he'd already factored into his plans?

Midge gestured at the ceiling. 'There was a terrific thunderstorm a few nights ago, and the heavy rain made the roof leak. We didn't realise until we found everything ruined the next morning and — ' She broke off as she noticed my expression. 'Is there a problem? Jack said — well, I got the feeling you were moving in with each other very soon.'

I slanted a poisonous look at Jack; but he avoided my gaze, evidently transfixed by something in the tree outside the window. My only option was to take matters into my own hands — or try to. I turned to Midge and said brightly, 'With Jack's cold, it would probably be best if I found a hotel.'

She frowned. 'You'll be lucky to get a room on a Friday night at this time of year.' Then, as if struck by a new idea, 'I've never known Jack have a summer cold — have you two had a tiff?'

'Yes,' I replied, just as he said, 'No.'

A peal of laughter from Midge. 'Go on, the pair of you! I'm sure you'll find a way to make up. And please use this bathroom,' she added, indicating a door at the end of the room. 'It wasn't affected by the leak, and it's a lot less basic than Hermann.' A knowing glance at each of us in turn. 'I'll leave you to sort yourselves out, we'll be in the garden.'

As soon as she'd gone downstairs, I hissed, 'What the hell do you think you're playing at?'

'I didn't know this room was out of action — '

'But implying that we're going to be living together — '

'What's wrong with that? If you're the only woman I've ever brought here, that would mean you're pretty special — and moving in together would be a natural next step.'

I glared at him. 'It's a totally hypothetical situation, of course, but I imagine one of us would have to change jobs first.'

'In the longer term, yes. But we could see each other at weekends even now.'

'No thanks. The thought of spending my free time in Grimshaw holds no appeal whatsoever.'

'Pity. To me, it wouldn't matter where we were — as long as we were together.' He picked up my case and made for the stairs, firing a parting shot over his shoulder — 'I'll be outside, waiting to show you our little love nest.'

I wrenched open the bathroom door. The compact luxury of what would have been my en suite went some way to restoring my equilibrium. But that ridiculous conversation about seeing each other every weekend played on my mind; it was as if we were discussing a real possibility — which didn't exist, and never would.

When I went downstairs again, Jack was leaning back against the front door as if to prevent my escape. I rattled the handle in annoyance, and he turned round slowly. His face wore an unusually bleak expression, and I suspected that he was still dwelling on my words of rejection — however theoretical they might be.

He opened the door and stood in the way, so that it was impossible to get past. 'There's something else I need to tell you.'

'Go ahead. It can't make things any worse than they already are.'

He cleared his throat. 'It's about Karina.'

Oh fantastic, just when I think it can't get any worse . . . He's going to confess that they're having an affair behind her boyfriend's back. And technically behind my back, as his new girlfriend. Not that I care, of course; not in the slightest.

'You probably realised in the restaurant that she's my ex,' he went on. 'She's been going out with a guy called Henrik, and now she's decided to break up with him.' He paused. 'To cut a long story short, she wants to be back with me. Trouble is, she's threatening to come up here this weekend so that we can talk things over.'

'Fine by me — although it might get a bit crowded in the motorhome,' I said, acidly.

A tight-lipped smile. 'Well, it's not fine by me. But having you as my girlfriend could be handy if she does turn up. With Karina, actions speak louder than words — and I need her to get the message.'

Which message? That he doesn't want her back — or, more likely, that she's got competition and she'll need to up her game?

Something he'd said earlier snagged in my mind, a flaw in his preposterous argument. 'How will she know where to find you, if you've never brought her here?' I narrowed my eyes. 'Unless, of course, you've given her this address, set it all up — '

'I have.'

The speed of his confession took me aback. 'You have?'

'Yes, I gave her Midge and Bill's address ages ago. She wanted to send them a card when they moved in.'

'Oh.'

'But I swear this isn't a set-up, Alicia. For all I know, she could be coming up the drive right now.'

I tilted my head to one side, as if giving the whole idea serious consideration. 'Let me get this right . . . You signed a contract for executive coaching. Perhaps you could show me where it specifies duties such as' — I checked them off on my fingers — 'pretending to be romantically involved . . . protecting you from your exes turning up inconveniently, which I imagine could be a full-time job in itself . . . and, last but by no means least, planning when we can set up home together!'

He stared down at me for several long seconds; then, before I could protest, he placed his hands on my shoulders. Firmly, so that I could feel their heat through the thin fabric of my T-shirt. 'Last night, at dinner, you said that reading up on my personal life gave you an insight into how I do business — remember?' I gave a non-committal nod, wondering where he was taking this. 'Well, I'm asking you — as my coach — to give me some support with a personal matter, only if it's needed, and only over the next two days. Will you do that, Alicia?'

I looked up at him, disconcerted. When he put it like that . . . well, how could I refuse? 'Okay, then,' I heard myself say slowly. 'But my warning about compromising situations still applies — '

'So does my word that you'll be safe with me.' As if to emphasise the point, he lifted his hands from my shoulders and stood back from the door to let me through. 'Come and meet Hermann.'

He walked off and I followed, struggling to match his long strides. 'I still don't see why we need to keep up the act in front of Bill and Midge,' I said in a stage whisper, as if they — or, heaven forbid, Karina — might be stalking us. 'Surely, if we explain, they'll understand?'

A frowning sidelong look. 'They will — but, as I've said, you won't get as much out of them. And this weekend is important for my coaching, isn't it?'

And for mine. The warmth of his touch, in the car and just now, was a poignant reminder of a time when I'd taken that sort of thing for granted. A time when I'd wholeheartedly embraced the instinctive intimacies, the unspoken permissions, of being in love. A time when . . .

I squared my shoulders, shook off the memories, pulled myself together.

Okay. This is for one weekend, no more than a couple of days — then I can disengage from coaching him, professionalism and dignity intact. So what if I also use it as a kind of physical and emotional 'rehab', an opportunity to clean old wounds in the hope that they'll finally heal? As for the man cast in the role of my lover, isn't it a no-brainer? Most women would give their right arm to be in my shoes . . .

We turned a corner — metaphorically perhaps, as well as literally — and arrived at a wooden-framed carport, its fresh blue paint decorated with red roses and yellow daisies in the style of a traditional narrow boat. A lovingly constructed shelter for the motorhome parked beneath it, large and white and — even to my untutored eye — eccentrically retro. Somehow I couldn't bring myself to call it Hermann; the name implied approval, even affection — and I was a long way from either.

But, as I went up the two steps and through the open door, that proved to be the least of my worries. After the sunlight, it took more than a moment to adjust to the relative gloom. Or was it because my eyes were immediately drawn to a bed that occupied almost the full length and width of the vehicle?

I suppressed a shiver and attempted a calm assessment of the situation. With its crisp white sheets and red-and-white patterned duvet, the bed looked almost inviting — and, more importantly, spacious enough to avoid unwanted familiarity. In fact, I reckoned I could construct a sturdy little wall down the middle, using the plump red cushions that formed an unofficial headboard. No chance of him 'accidentally' invading my half, with that in place.

I stepped down from the motorhome. 'It's okay, I suppose. We shouldn't be on top of one another.' An unfortunate turn of phrase, and I blushed.

He raised one eyebrow. 'Only if we both want to be.'

'You know that's not going to happen,' I said, frostily.

'But it helps to imagine it could, since we're supposed to be in a physical relationship.' He held out his hand. 'Let's at least pretend we've kissed and made up before you meet Bill — he's the main reason we're here, after all.'

I stared at his hand with its clean long lines and no rings. *Deep breath.*

And another. Oh, for God's sake — just do it! On impulse, I let go of my misgivings and slipped my hand into his. More yielding than our business handshakes, but I steeled myself against the spark. So far, so good. I looked up, and tried out a doting smile.

'Wow, an Oscar-winning performance.' That wicked grin resurfaced, transforming him into someone I might actually enjoy spending the weekend with.

Which isn't the point at all.

We strolled into the garden — a tangle of shrubs and roses, their colour and profusion contained by a network of gravel paths and low walls. Birdsong rippled through the sultry air, pure and mellow. Before us, tawny red in the evening sun, a steep hillside rose to a high serrated ridge.

Jack's grip on my hand tightened as he steered me towards the murmur of voices, through an arch of wide-eyed white roses and onto a slate patio. Here we found Midge at a wrought-iron table contemplating two bottles of wine, and Bill — a tall, bulky man with a greying beard — tending a barbecue.

'At last,' she said. 'I was about to send a search party!' An appraising look. 'You're friends again, thank goodness. Let me get you both a glass of wine.'

Bill put down his tongs and came towards us. A hearty clasp of hands with Jack, a hug and kiss for me. Ironic, wasn't it, that I was allowing more affection from his friends than I would ever allow from him?

'Sit here, Alicia.' Midge patted the seat nearest to her. 'White or red?'

I hesitated — wasn't I working? But it seemed churlish to refuse, and I resolved to make one glass last all evening. 'White, thank you.'

Jack sat down on my other side. 'Are you warm enough, love?'

It took a moment to realise he was talking to me. 'Oh — yes.' To disguise my embarrassment, I blurted out the first thing that came into my head. 'What a lovely place, I wish we were staying for longer.'

His arm snaked along the back of my chair. 'So do I.'

'But we can't,' I said firmly, with a warning look in his direction.

'Next time, then,' Midge said. 'Especially now that Jack's remembered his way here.'

Bill chuckled. 'What she means, Alicia, is that he hasn't been to see us for a while. I've a feeling that we have you to thank for this visit.'

'True, except that we did have an ulterior motive.' A coy smile at Jack.

He smiled back, but cautiously. 'We did?'

'Yes.' I paused. Served him right if he thought I was going to confess about the coaching and abandon the role play. 'You thought staying with Bill and Midge would make my first trip to the Lake District a success, whatever the weather — remember?'

Our eyes met. Perhaps he detected the triumph in mine, because he lifted his arm from the back of my chair and casually ran his fingertip across the bare skin of my neck. Unexpected, and totally unnecessary. I flinched, then tried to cover up with, 'Don't — you know how ticklish I am.'

His finger moved instantly from my neck, only to resurface at the small of my back where my T-shirt had pulled away from my jeans. I nearly jumped out of my chair. 'I certainly do,' he said, blandly.

'Och, leave the poor girl alone,' Midge said. 'You've plenty of time for that later.'

I leaned back in my chair, slamming his hand against the wrought iron.

'I'm feeling well and truly crushed,' he said, in that black-velvet voice. 'But I'm sure it won't last.'

Midge handed round some olives. 'Jack told us you were from the south, Alicia — whereabouts?'

'Hampshire. I still live there — a little place called Helsingham, just off the M3.'

'But you met Jack up north — was it

something to do with work? He was a wee bit vague about that part on the phone.'

'Hardly surprising.' A glance of malicious sweetness at Jack. 'We met at the ballet.'

'The ballet?' Bill looked as though he wasn't sure whether to be amused or alarmed.

'Yes, I was in Manchester to see a client, and managed to get a ticket for *Les Sylphides*. Jack was sitting next to me, we got talking and — well, the rest is history, as they say.'

'Not quite,' Jack said, extricating his hand at last — only to rest it on my knee, rather too heavily. 'You missed out the bit where you tried to squeeze past me without waking me up. You got stuck in a very interesting position — far more entertaining than the ballet, actually.'

They all laughed, and I forced myself to join in.

'I'd have fallen asleep, too,' Bill said. 'What possessed you to go in the first place?'

'We can't even get you to the theatre in Keswick,' Midge put in. Then, turning to me, 'It's in a beautiful setting right on the lake, well worth a visit — maybe the next time you're up?'

'Of course.' I suppressed a twinge of guilt; little did she realise that this 'relationship' was heading for the rocks as soon as the weekend was over.

She beamed at me. 'Good. As soon as you let me know a date, I'll book us in — we can leave these two philistines in the pub for the evening. But Jack — *you* at the ballet? Was this some sort of Billy Elliot moment?'

'Not exactly — the Northern Ballet approached Leo Components for sponsorship and gave me complimentary tickets, so I agreed to go along. In the end, I couldn't persuade the Board to go ahead with the sponsorship — but otherwise it turned out to be one of the best decisions I've ever made.' His eyes sought mine, their expression unbelievably adoring, while I made a mental note of how easily he could conjure up a plausible story.

I held his gaze just long enough to appear equally besotted, before saying, 'Luckily for me, you were on your own that night. And for once we didn't bump into any of your exes.'

A grunt from Midge. 'I can't imagine Karina going anywhere just to be in the audience, she's more of a centre-stage person.'

Oh, not Karina again. I glanced across at Jack, barely concealing my resentment. *It's always about* her *— as though no one else exists. What about all the others?*

'Karina's the past,' Jack said, softly. 'Alicia's my future.' And, before I could snatch it away, he reached for my hand and lifted it to his lips.

As a kiss, it was nothing — a little charade hardly worthy of my reaction — yet at the same time it was everything. A breach in the many-layered wall I'd built round me since Troy. A threat to the control with which I lived my life. And something even more worrying — because part of me didn't want to snatch my hand away at all.

When at last he lowered my hand from his lips, he kept it curled within his. In the still of the evening, my pulse raced. It might only be role play, but the effects were unnervingly real.

Bill was asking me about my job. In my confusion, I blurted out, 'I'm an executive coach.'

'Oh?' Midge leaned forward, while Jack's grip on my hand tightened, ever so slightly. 'What does that involve?'

'Helping organisations to get the best out of their senior management,' I said, seizing my chance to inject a bigger shot of truth into this escalating fantasy world.

A bark of laughter from Bill. 'Maybe Jack could recommend you to Leo Components.'

'Funny you should say that.' A pause, to let Jack sweat a little. 'We were talking about something similar on the way here — weren't we, *darling*? Only problem is,' — a resigned sigh — 'I couldn't possibly date one of my clients. Conflict of interest and all that.'

'Too right,' Jack said quickly. 'If it comes down to having Alicia as my girlfriend or my coach, then give me the girlfriend every time.' His eyes danced, as if goading me to respond — or at least enjoy the irony.

Terrier-like, Midge persisted with the earlier subject. 'And how long have you two been together? Jack was vague about that, as well.'

The question caught me off guard. Even in a totally hypothetical situation, I wouldn't have gone away for the weekend with him this early. It was only the second time we'd met, for God's sake. I plucked a figure out of thin air and replied, 'Two months' — just as Jack said, 'A couple of weeks.' I raised my eyebrows at him as if to say, 'Get yourself out of *that*.' He went on, 'We've only been, er, close for a couple of weeks, although of course Alicia's right — we met almost two months ago.'

Close? In other words, having sex. Huh, in his dreams. I picked up my glass with my free hand, and yanked the other from his grasp on the pretext of taking an olive. Then, with all physical contact broken, I redirected the conversation to safer territory. 'Where are we going tomorrow? I can't wait to do some hillwalking.'

'It'll depend on the forecast.' Jack looked across at Midge and Bill. 'Which is . . . ?'

'I'll go into Keswick first thing in the morning,' Bill said, 'and look at the local forecast outside the Moot Hall. That one's far more reliable than anyone else's. If it's good, we thought we'd go up Skidder with a picnic lunch. Is that okay with you, Alicia?'

'Sounds wonderful — except I'd better reserve judgement until I know what going up Skidder means.'

'It's the local name for Skiddaw,' Jack said. 'Fourth highest peak in the Lakes after the Scafells and Helvellyn.'

A moment of panic at the mention of

‘fourth highest’. *Can I fabricate a dodgy ankle? Too late — I should have used that as an excuse right at the start.* ‘Is it, um, much of a climb? I’m not a big fan of heights.’

Bill gave me a reassuring grin. ‘Don’t worry, it’s not too bad. No nasty ridges like Helvellyn, or Blencathra behind us.’

‘You’ll be fine, love,’ Jack added, with a mischievous grin. ‘We both know you’re a slave to the gym.’

Fantastic; not only am I pretending to be his current bedmate throughout the weekend — I’m also having to act as if I’m super fit. At this precise moment, I’m not sure which will be the bigger challenge.

‘Let’s eat,’ Midge said. ‘Come to the kitchen, both of you, and give me a hand to carry the food out. Five minutes, Bill?’

‘Aye, the meat’s all cooked, I’m just letting it rest.’

It was a surprisingly relaxed meal, in the shadow of Blencathra, among the heady scents of an English garden at the close of a sun-drenched day. I asked Bill about his work, to establish an unobtrusive springboard for further discussions. But I didn't force the issue, especially when Midge started to talk about the latest exploits of some of the village characters. As she had the timing of a born comic, her anecdotes made for plenty of laughter.

Darkness fell swiftly — or perhaps I was too engrossed in the conversation to notice it enveloping us. Time to bring today's deception to an end and try out the motorhome, with all *that* would involve. Even though I wasn't expecting Jack to hit on me, the prospect of being alone with him in a confined space — in a bed, for God's sake! — filled me with apprehension.

I finished my wine and got to my feet. 'Let me help with the clearing up, then I'll say goodnight.'

Midge insisted, however, that they could manage; next thing I knew, I was walking hand in hand with Jack through the garden. The sky was a tapestry of tiny stars, the moon pinned against it like a giant pearl. I was too busy looking up to watch my step; inevitable, then, that I tripped and almost fell . . .

It had been so long since I'd let a man hold me this close — how could it feel natural? Yet, in the cradle of his arms, I felt my body shiver at the haunting memory of physical and emotional need. In an act of pure self-preservation, I buried my face in his shoulder. Because, whereas an embrace could be construed as an instinctive move to break my fall, a kiss would spell disaster.

Not that I *would ever kiss* him — *but he might be tempted to try it*.

'Are you okay?' His voice in the darkness was soft as a caress.

'Of course,' I lied.

He released me, gently but firmly, sought my hand again, and we continued through the garden. After a moment, he said, 'Your stumble was well timed. Midge appeared, saw us, and turned back. If *she* didn't want to disturb us, it must have looked like a convincing clinch.'

I couldn't think of a reply but, as we reached the motorhome, my heart started to pound. Putting on a show for the others — intentionally or otherwise — was one thing; spending the next ten hours or so in enforced intimacy was an entirely different matter.

He opened the door, leaned in to switch on the light, and hung back to let me go in. When I glanced over my shoulder to see if he was following, he said, 'I think I'll have a nightcap with Midge and Bill — give you some privacy.'

My stomach churned; relief and, in a strange way, disappointment. I spun round, veiling my confusion with a sardonic laugh. 'Won't they think it's odd that you're not exactly — well, jumping into bed with me? Aren't we still at that stage in our relationship?'

'We certainly are. But we're both tired — and anyway, there's always the morning.'

Oh God, does he have even that worked out?

I fumbled desperately for a different

subject. 'Midge and Bill are good company. I like them very much.'

'They like you very much too. I can tell.' A pause. 'You know, tonight went better than I'd dared hope.'

'In spite of the ballet?'

A wry smile. 'In spite of the ballet. Although I'm already thinking how to pay you back for that.'

'Didn't you get your revenge by making me out to be — how did you put it? — a slave to the gym? That'll take some living up to tomorrow.'

'Doubt it, you look in good shape to me.'

An echo of the first time we met, when his eyes had told me the same thing — except he'd gone on to apologise for it. And later he'd informed Nick Suggett that I wasn't his type — but then tried to deny it. Why did it matter whether he found me attractive? I was adding a totally unnecessary complication to an already difficult relationship . . .

His low chuckle interrupted my attack of self-reproach. 'You know, it felt weird when you said you'd never date one of your clients. My first thought was — hang on, I *am* your client.'

'But we're not dating, are we?' I countered, swiftly. 'Anyway, *you* said something just as weird — that you didn't want me as your coach. Not so long ago you said the exact opposite.'

'What I said tonight was — if it's a choice between having you as my girlfriend or my coach, then give me the girlfriend every time. That's not necessarily a contradiction with saying I want you as my coach, is it?' His voice was soft, and flirtatious, and for a moment I almost believed him. Which would have been a really stupid thing to do.

Hoping that he wouldn't see my blushes, I mumbled a goodnight and turned away. Behind me the door closed, leaving me alone with my trepidation.

I had enjoyed the evening far more than I'd expected to — and that meant I had to be even more on my guard tomorrow. Always assuming, of course, that I got through tonight.

8

I woke up with a start. Something was wrong — in fact, everything was wrong. Strange room, strange bed; and — worst of all — the feeling that I wasn't alone.

Then I remembered: this was the motorhome, and I was in bed with Jack Smith. *But of course it's not* that *sort of 'in bed with' — is it?* I risked a look to my right. Thank God, the barrier of cushions was still intact; I'd constructed it last night, as soon as I'd been to the bathroom and changed into my pyjamas. I'd struggled to get to sleep, expecting him to walk through the door at any moment. But it hadn't happened and, in the end, I must have drifted off.

Everything was warm and peaceful and morning-light. I lifted the edge of the curtain and found the sun already climbing the sky. Above me, unseen, a wood pigeon chuntered a good-natured greeting. I groped for my watch on the shelf behind my head. Six fifty-five. If it hadn't been for the man beyond the cushions, I'd have enjoyed a lie-in. But I'd slept surprisingly well; and, anyway, it was safer to be somewhere else when he awoke.

Slowly, stealthily, I peeled back my half of the duvet and sat up. The bed was enclosed on three sides by walls, two of them external and one a partition to divide the sleeping quarters from the galley kitchen. Last night I'd got in at the only accessible side and settled myself next to the window, so that he wouldn't have to climb over me when he came to bed. But that was when he wasn't there; this morning was an entirely different matter.

I knelt on the duvet and started at the bottom of the wall of cushions, carefully dismantling them one by one. When I reached the middle, I gave him a furtive look. His face wore the mask of sleep, but I didn't want to push my luck — and there was now enough room for me to get off the bed. I took a deep breath and clambered silently over his legs, watching him closely in case he stirred. Mid-straddle was *not* a good look.

It was as if he'd read my mind. His eyes flicked open and taunted mine, briefly, before travelling casually downwards; here and there they lingered, making me painfully aware of my too-skimpy pyjamas. And, throughout it all, I was incapable of moving — a real 'rabbit in the headlights' moment.

At last he looked up, his grin wide and wicked. 'So dreams can come true.'

I almost vaulted off the bed and scurried to the door, snatching up my sponge bag and a handful of clothes to cover my semi-nakedness. I realised I was trembling — with anger at myself and at him, of course; and with something else, something that I couldn't bring myself to acknowledge. But all I could say was a feeble, 'Do you *mind*?'

He propped himself on his elbows,

and I noted his bare shoulders and chest. In fact, I found myself wondering whether he was wearing anything at all . . . Once again, as if in tune with my thoughts, his grin broadened. 'I don't mind in the least, I'm just sorry that we can't take advantage of the situation. Unless we change the rules, of course.'

An image of limbs entwined, his and mine, mouths chasing kisses; I felt my face burn. 'I'm going to the bathroom.'

'With my shirt? I'm touched.'

I dropped the clothes as if they were hot coals, grabbed what I needed from my suitcase and fled.

Up in the bathroom, a period of reflection and a hot shower eased some of my mortification. After all, things could have been a lot worse. Apart from that embarrassing encounter as I climbed over him, my first night with Jack Smith had been uneventful; and, strangely, the prospect of a day on the hills with him and his friends rather appealed.

When I returned to the motorhome,

he was nowhere to be seen. I hesitated, then arranged the cushions along the headboard and straightened the duvet, so that Midge wouldn't suspect anything if she looked in.

Let the role play recommence.

I found everyone busy in the kitchen: Bill frying bacon and eggs, Midge making a tower of sandwiches and Jack — well, I couldn't say what he was doing because, as soon as he saw me, he came straight over and took me in his arms.

'Mmm, you smell good,' he said, loud enough for the others to hear.

I forced myself to cling to him, briefly, before wriggling free. 'So does breakfast.'

'How do you like your eggs, Alicia?' Bill said.

'Turned over, please. Can I do anything?'

Midge looked up and grinned. 'Help Jack with the tea and toast — he seems to have lost the plot now that you're here. Or would you prefer coffee?'

'Tea's fine, thank you.' I followed Jack across the kitchen and got to grips with the toaster while he filled the kettle. We worked side by side, in what must have looked like an amicable silence; in reality, I was all too aware of his nearness. The natural scent of him — unwashed male in yesterday's clothes — wasn't off-putting; quite the opposite. Yet another problem for me to deal with.

After breakfast, while Jack went off to get ready, Bill brought out some maps and showed me our route. First, we were going up a small hill called Latrigg, as a warm-up exercise for its neighbour, Skiddaw. He warned me that Skiddaw itself would be a tougher walk, except that perseverance would be rewarded: the views from the summit should be spectacular.

The map, of course, was not the territory — but the map looked terrifying enough. I bit my lip; it looked as though my 'slave to the gym' fitness levels would be well and truly put to the test.

'I checked the forecast in Keswick earlier, and we're in for a warm day,' Bill went on. 'Unfortunately, that means carrying extra water.'

'As well as one of Midge's special packed lunches?' This from Jack, strolling into the room in khaki combat shorts and a maroon T-shirt. 'God help us, we'll be like a pair of packhorses.'

Bill chuckled. 'I've got a couple of framed rucksacks we can use — then at least we'll be well equipped pack-horses.'

Packhorses? Although I joined in the laughter, I was privately reflecting that Jack looked more like a prize stallion. As before, seeing him in casual clothes made me feel hot and formal. For a moment, I debated whether to switch my cropped navy trousers for the pair of shorts I'd brought with me; then decided I'd had enough of Jack ogling my legs for one day. Except that now, I realised uncomfortably, it was more a case of me ogling his.

We set off from the cottage around

quarter to ten — heading westwards along a narrow lane. The sun was already beating down and I was grateful for the floppy hat Midge had lent me. She and I walked together, maintaining a steady pace and an equally well-judged conversation. She asked me about my family, a subject I found I could handle without any subterfuge whatsoever. I talked to her about my parents carving out a new life for themselves in Spain, and my sister relocating to Canada with her husband.

'And soon you'll be settling down with Jack, by the sound of it,' she put in.

'Oh, I don't know about that.' Maybe I sounded too horrified, because she turned her head and gave me a penetrating look. 'It's early days,' I added, lamely.

'Not necessarily. I can tell he's serious.'

Huh, more like a bloody good actor!

She continued, 'You make a great couple. I haven't seen him like this for years — so at ease with himself.'

Oh, please. At this rate she'll have us engaged before the weekend's over . . .

'It's probably the merger with Sphinx,' I said, quickly. 'Being Chief Exec of a bigger company seems to motivate him.'

'Alicia, believe me, it's nothing to do with work — he's always been good at keeping his personal life separate. This weekend, with you, he seems . . . happy.' The implication was that this was something unusual.

'Wasn't he happy with Karina?' The question was out before I could determine the pros and cons of hearing the reply.

A pause. 'What's he told you about her?'

'Nothing specific — but I've seen the impact she still has on him. She came over to us at Corleone's on Thursday night, and — and he took her home.' That much was accurate, as was the disapproval in my voice.

'Was she drunk?'

'A little, I suppose.'

'Well then, there's your answer.'

But it wasn't quite the answer I wanted. And I couldn't pursue it any further because Jack came up behind us and said, 'My turn now, Midge. In any case, your husband needs you for moral support — I've just been giving him an earbashing about Lauren.'

'Och, just when we were getting to the interesting bits about you.' A stage whisper in my direction — 'See what I mean? He just can't stay away!' — before she drew to one side of the lane to wait for Bill.

Jack grabbed my hand and stepped up the pace. When we were at a safe distance from the others, he said, 'I thought you needed rescuing.'

'Thanks, but I didn't. Who's Lauren?'

'Their daughter. She's at university, but Bill's still very protective.' A pause. 'Don't you want to know the real reason for interrupting your conversation with Midge?'

'No, although I have a feeling you're going to tell me all the same.'

'I couldn't handle the view for much longer.'

I frowned. 'The view?'

'You in those trousers.'

A sidelong glance, in case he was joking; but his expression was enigmatic. When I tried to wrench my hand away, he held it tight — and I didn't want to make a scene in front of our distant witnesses.

Instead, I said sharply, 'You're overdoing the role play, aren't you, with that sort of comment? Especially as nobody can hear.'

He stopped dead, startling me into doing the same. I looked straight at him, trying in vain to detect the tiniest gleam of malice in his eyes; strange how the habit of self-preservation plays out.

Then he said softly, 'Where does the role play end and the real play begin?'

His question gave me goosebumps, in spite of the heat. It summed up my dilemma completely: by agreeing to this charade of a relationship, I was subjecting myself to a form of behavioural therapy.

The flooding process, to be exact: putting myself into the very situation I feared and forcing myself to confront it head on. Of course, the flooding process would end with the visit to Bill and Midge — but what about everything else? I wasn't even certain what 'everything else' entailed; I just hoped that it was the revival of old memories and not the creation of new ones.

'Come on,' he said, 'before the others catch us up.'

We walked on, still — bizarrely — holding hands, deep in our own thoughts. From time to time he broke the silence with some observation or other, but I kept my responses brief and unencouraging. As the surrounding fields and woods gave way to a grassy hillside, I focused on where I was placing my feet; no way was I going to trip into his arms like the night before. Only when we reached the cairn on Latrigg's summit did I lift my head and take a proper look at the world around me.

My God. Now I could see why they'd

brought me here.

Far below us, like the discarded plaything of a child-giant, sparkled a miniature land — an oasis in a rock-strewn desert. Two shimmering sapphire lakes, studded with tiny boats; along their edges, dense woods and roads jewelled with cars; between them, a jumble of gunmetal roofs and emerald lawns. And rising above all of this, on a scale that took my breath away, the hills.

Involuntarily, as if I needed to register this intense feeling of awe, my hand tightened round Jack's. I sensed him glance at me, then look away. Silence welled between us, different from before, almost companionable; at least on my part.

In the end Jack released my hand, rummaged in his rucksack and handed me a bottle of water. I held it to my chest, enjoying the sudden chill, but didn't drink immediately; the view slaked a thirst I didn't know I had.

'Derwentwater on the left, Bassenthwaite Lake on the right.' His voice, too close. 'Keswick in the middle, a tourist trap all year round. Whereas up here . . . '

In one sweeping gesture his arm embraced the summit, marking the contrast. I could see no more than a scattering of people, including Bill and Midge some distance away, with their backs to us. Their joined hands spoke of being there for each other, year after year — unlike Jack's and mine.

But I miss his touch, however fake.

A deep breath to steady my thoughts. I let my eyes feast on the hills, huge crested grey-brown waves rolling to meet the blue-domed sky. The last time I'd seen nature at its most majestic with a man at my side was California; and majesty had soon turned to misery . . . I gave the bottle cap a frantic twist and took a long gulp of water.

Beside me, Jack was unpacking a couple of sandwiches. When he offered me one, I took it, surprised that I could be hungry so soon after breakfast. As we ate, his hand came to rest on my shoulder, too firm to shrug off.

When we'd finished, he said, 'Let me introduce you to some of the northern fells.' His voice softened with pride. 'If you look straight up from that furthermost island on Derwentwater,' — he stooped until his head was level with mine; and pointed, so that there was no mistaking — 'you'll see Maiden Moor and Dale Head, then Hindscarth and Pillar. And in front, the one like a cat crouching — that's Catbells. Beyond it is the Newlands Valley, home of Mrs Tiggy-Winkle.'

His last words were so incongruous that I burst out laughing.

'So my mother always told me.' He grinned, and gave my shoulder an affectionate squeeze — for Bill and Midge's benefit, of course.

'That was one of my favourite books.' I let slip a nostalgic sigh. 'I used to walk round the garden pretending to be Lucie with my pocket handkin.'

'You're a Beatrix Potter fan, but you've never visited the Lakes before?'

His astonishment put me instantly on the defensive. 'I grew up on the south coast, and my parents wanted to spend as little of their leisure time as possible in the car. Our UK holidays tended to be in the New Forest, or Devon and Cornwall.'

'I suppose I should be grateful that most southerners do the same, otherwise the Lakes would be even busier.' He paused to scan the land around us. 'The best of my childhood was spent here. My parents used to bring us every year, until I was thirteen or fourteen.'

'Us' implied he had a sibling; brother or sister, one or more? Not that I needed to know anything about his family, or his childhood, unless it was relevant to his work. But, just when I was about to ask, his hand slid effortlessly from my shoulder to my hip, and under my T-shirt.

'Get *off*!' I said, through gritted teeth.

The hand didn't move. 'I'm just behaving in character. You could at least pretend to respond, like you did last night in the garden.'

'I did no such thing! I just — '

'Come on, Alicia, don't you remember what it's like?'

'What what's like?'

'To be at this stage of a relationship.' Somehow I was in his arms, hands flat against his chest but making no attempt to push him away. My eyes locked unwillingly with his; blue depths, green flecks — a natural harmony with the scene below. He went on, his voice low and compelling, 'You want to touch each other all the time and you can't help showing it . . . Each touch builds a memory, each memory builds a need . . . And when you're standing here, in one of the most perfect places on earth, on a perfect day — doesn't it remind you of our other perfect moments? Such as this morning, when we made love — because we would have done, if this was real play not role play . . . And we link the moments, and the memories, like this.'

His fingertips feathered the skin at

the small of my back. Traitorous skin, trembling as if in recollection of an earlier, more intimate touch. Traitorous hands, stealing round his neck, bringing his mouth close enough to —

I pulled away just in time, and stumbled out of his reach. 'I can't do this.'

'It looked a pretty good performance from where I was standing.' His tone was flat, the words matter-of-fact, the spell broken.

'But an unnecessary one. I don't do public displays of affection, I'm not that type. And another thing, I need to start a discussion with Bill soon — otherwise I'm just wasting my time this weekend.'

'Thanks.' He turned his back on me, picked up the rucksack.

'I meant professionally speaking.'

'I'm sure you did.' The rucksack swung heavily onto his shoulders. 'Trust me, you'll need all your concentration for climbing Skiddaw. Leave Bill until tonight, or tomorrow.'

I stared unseeingly in the direction of the hill shaped like a crouching cat.

Didn't he realise that my job was the only reason I was here? Otherwise I'd be safe at home, enjoying my own space and my own life —

'Are you ready to go on, Alicia?' Midge's voice behind me, edged with concern.

I fixed a bright smile in place and spun around. 'Of course.'

Little did she know that her question was open to an entirely different interpretation.

9

Whether by accident or design, Jack walked on ahead with Midge. I could see from the set of his shoulders, and her frequent frowning glances up at him, that their conversation was not a happy one. Part of me longed to know what they were saying, the other part relished the opportunity to interview Bill.

I started by asking him about his plans for the future, and whether they included a permanent move to the Lakes. From there, it was a simple step to a discussion about work and how he'd met Jack. Like most of my clients, he was eager to talk business with a sympathetic listener.

At first, I felt I was making little headway; we seemed to be mired down in reminiscences from the early years of their relationship. Then, almost as an aside, he said, 'Not that I'd expect anything else, after what happened to his father.'

'Ye-es,' I said tentatively, wondering if this was something I would be expected to know.

'He'll have told you all about it, of course.'

'Mmm.'

'When I heard the Sphinx announcement, I thought he was stark staring mad.'

'Did you?'

'Wouldn't *you*?'

'I'm not sure — '

'Watch your step here.' He paused while we both negotiated a particularly steep incline. 'I mean — dredging it all up again, trying to right old wrongs.'

'I suppose so,' I said, hoping that this was a suitable response. Once again, I sensed that whatever had happened to Jack's father was significant, although what it had to do with Sphinx I couldn't imagine.

'He won't admit it, but I know that's

what he's doing.'

He stopped — and so did I, welcoming the chance to catch my breath as unobtrusively as I could. While he adjusted his rucksack, I stared ahead at Jack. He scaled the rocky path without any apparent effort: a study in strength and stamina, the fluid movements and easy balance of an athlete, pausing only to offer Midge a helping hand. Yet what I'd just learnt suggested even greater vulnerability than I'd detected from our dealings so far . . .

I sensed, rather than heard, that Bill had asked me a question. 'Sorry?'

'I said, don't you see this all the time in your job? Isn't that why people employ a coach — to rectify something in their past?'

'I prefer to think of it as earning themselves a better future.'

'Maybe, maybe not. Here, we'd better get moving — those two are nearly at the top.'

I sighed and made a mental note of all he'd told me; writing it down would have to wait. When at last we joined the others, Jack herded me to one side with the excuse of naming more hills. It was also, of course, an opportunity for him to wind his arm around my waist, pull me close and murmur, 'How was your little talk with Bill?'

'Very enlightening,' I said, coolly.

'Oh?' A less playful tone now.

'We need to discuss it somewhere else, in case I'm tempted to push you off this mountain.' I looked up at him with a deceptively loving smile. 'And how was your little talk with Midge?'

A rueful laugh, as his eyes clashed with mine. 'Very . . . belittling. One of her specials — if I didn't know better, I'd have thought you put her up to it. You both have the same knack of making me feel two feet tall.'

'What was she belittling you about?'

He paused, then fixed his gaze on the hills opposite. 'She's worried that there's some tension between us, that we've still not made up from our tiff yesterday — or, at least, not properly.' A pause;

then he added, 'And she thinks I'd be a bloody fool to let you get away.'

It was spoken half to himself, as if I wasn't meant to hear. Which, strangely, made it all the more heartfelt. Pink-cheeked, I said the first thing that came into my head. 'Sounds like we've managed to convince her that this is a real relationship.'

'Not quite.' A slow deep breath, his gaze still distant. 'Which is why we need to put on a bit more of a show.'

Then he turned to me, tightened his grip on my waist and cupped my face with his other hand, his lips blotting out my yelp of protest. A kiss of affection rather than passion, thank God. So why did part of me yearn for something more?

Before my mouth could betray me, he gently brought the kiss to an end. And I . . . I rested my head on his shoulder and closed my eyes. An attitude of contentment, belying the turmoil inside.

Because it had taken only a split

second, a micro moment, to undo the work of three years. Oh, I'd had a kiss or two since Troy — pathetic little triumphs of anger, hurt and revenge, futile attempts to salve my wounds. *But this was different, totally different. And it wasn't even a proper kiss . . . Is that why? Is it the very absence of passion in the kisser that creates a need for it in the kissed?*

Oh God. How am I going to get through this weekend . . .

When I opened my eyes, the world was still as it had been: bright and big and beautiful. Only my view of it had changed.

At last, he broke the silence. 'Shall we join the others?'

'Yes.' It was little more than a whisper.

His arm steered me over to a shelf of rock where Bill and Midge had spread a rug. And somehow I sat and talked and ate and drank like a functioning human being. When I'd made enough inroads into the pile of sandwiches to please

Midge, it seemed natural to shift my position slightly, lean back against Jack and link his fingers through mine. Playing my part to perfection, as it were.

Except . . . where does the role play end and the real play begin?

From up here we could see a vaster spread of hills and, while Bill and Midge went for a stroll, he told me their names. Once again, I was mesmerised by the quaint words. *Or is it the lilt of his voice in my ear, the heat of his body behind me, the touch of his hand in mine?* Whereas the enchantment of Latrigg had been its panoramic surroundings, here on Skiddaw I was under a different spell . . .

'Next time,' he said, 'we'll climb Blencathra — '

'Next time?'

'Don't you want there to be a next time?'

'But we both know there won't be.'

'That's not what I asked.'

He was right, of course; but I wasn't going to give him an answer — and certainly not the one he wanted. I stared unseeingly across the valley.

'Alicia.'

'Yes.'

'Who was he?'

'Who?'

'The man who screwed you up.'

He made it sound so simple, when it was anything but. A pause, while I debated my reply; in the end I said slowly, 'Nobody screwed me up.'

'Oh, for fu — '

'I did it to myself. He — the man — was just — just an accessory.'

'So why can't you *un*do it to yourself?'

I gave a brittle laugh and twisted round to face him. 'Why can't *you* undo what you're doing to yourself?'

His jaw dropped. 'What *I'm* doing —?'

'Yes, changing your women more frequently than your underwear. Oh, and sleeping with your ex in between.'

'Is that what you think of me?'

'Why are you so surprised? I've read the local papers, seen you rush off with

Karina as soon as her boyfriend's back was turned — '

'You're making too many assumptions.' His tone was clipped, his eyes cold. 'And you know what they say about the word 'assume' — '

'One more thing,' I went on, interrupting the challenge; after all, I'd have been astonished if he'd agreed with me. 'Why did you *really* convince the Board to buy Sphinx Industries?' I lowered my voice, aware of Bill and Midge heading in our direction. 'Could it be anything to do with your father?'

He blinked, as if the taunt had struck home; but he didn't say a word. It was I who broke off the eye contact — jumping to my feet, scooping up the empty water bottles and kneeling down to stuff them into the nearest rucksack; any excuse to put some distance between us.

'Here, let me give you a hand.' Midge knelt beside me, and I forced myself to match her methodical movements. When the remnants of our picnic were neatly stowed in the rucksacks, she said, 'And how have you found your first Lakeland outing?'

Hardly a difficult question; but I took my time to formulate the right answer, leaning back on my heels, letting my gaze drift to Jack. He was now standing several yards away with Bill, dark head bent over the map. 'You know, it's had a totally unexpected effect on me. A sort of therapy . . . giving me a sense of perspective about the past, and the present.'

'And the future?'

I looked at her, trying to fathom out her agenda. 'That's not entirely within my control.'

'Not entirely, but a lot will depend on what you want and how much you want it.'

She'd shifted the conversation beyond my comfort zone; I made a last attempt to recover it. 'Believe me, I'm well acquainted with the process of goal setting.'

'Your head might be acquainted with it, Alicia, but what about your heart?'

she said, a sudden smile softening her words. Before I could reply, she stood up and called the men over to start the descent.

And then, to make matters worse, she kept Bill back — supposedly to help her remove a pebble from her shoe — which left me with Jack, and a strained silence.

When he strode on ahead, I thought he was just being rude. As I marched angrily in his wake, however, he turned and held out his hand. 'Best if I go first down this bit,' he said quietly, not even looking at me. I brushed his hand aside, lost my balance, skidded on the dry stony earth — and clutched at him to break my fall.

Was it the eagerness of his arms, or my half-hysterical giggle, or a potent combination of both? Whatever the catalyst, we clung to each other — and *laughed*. Body-shaking, glad-to-be-alive laughter that I didn't want to end. Or maybe I didn't want any of it to end.

A brisk 'Excuse me' brought us to

our senses, and we stepped aside to let an elderly couple go past. But as soon as they'd gone his hand found mine, and held it tight.

'I suppose I ought to thank you for saving my life,' I said, still breathless.

He looked down at me, shaking his head in mock bewilderment. 'Oh Alicia, what am I going to do with you? You'd rather throw yourself down Skidder than put your trust in me.'

'Point taken.' I tried a lungful of air, and grimaced. 'Ouch! Even though I didn't fall, you'll be glad to know I'm aching all over.'

A suggestive grin. 'Anything I can rub better?'

Several images came to mind, all of them compromising for an executive coach and her client. I fixed my gaze on the scuffed toes of my trainers. 'It's just — well, it's been a long time since I laughed like that, and my ribs hurt. I must be out of practice.'

'Me too,' he said. 'But it felt good, didn't it? Maybe it was an outlet,' he added in an undertone. 'After all, we were asking each other some difficult questions earlier.'

I jerked my head up in alarm. 'Jack, I'm meant to be doing the deep dive on you — not the other way round.'

'I know, and you'll get your answers. But there's a time and a place — and it's not here.' He let go of me to nudge his rucksack into a more comfortable position, then took my hand again. 'Come on, before Midge and Bill catch us up.'

So we walked, side by side whenever the path allowed; and we talked, sticking to safer ground — art, music and Italy. Only once did I make any reference to our role play, when I asked him if he thought we'd convinced Midge yet.

'That we're a couple, or that we've made up?' he said, raising his eyebrows.

'Both.'

'Probably. For a start, she's not bending my ear like she did on the way up.'

'Oh?' I prompted, as if I hadn't noticed.

'Let's just say she's on your side. She and Bill have really taken to you.' He gave a loud sigh.

'You sound surprised.'

A sidelong glance, his amusement obvious. 'Not so much surprised as disappointed. No, make that scared stiff — just imagine all the grief I'll get from her if we break up.'

It was more a case of 'when' than 'if', but I didn't bother to correct him. Instead, I steered the conversation to safer ground again.

We reached the cottage well before Midge and Bill; but, since Jack had the spare key, we could at least use the shower. I suggested he went first, while I stayed in the motorhome. I wanted to write up the notes from my interview with Bill and outline the next phase of questioning. Since I felt more like curling up and going to sleep, this proved to be quite a challenge; so much for the stamina of a gym slave.

I'd just packed away my notebook when Jack returned. In an instant the motorhome seemed disturbingly cramped, and in a panic I scrambled off the bed. He waited, all clean and fresh in cream chinos and a dark green shirt, while I rummaged in my suitcase for a change of clothes. On impulse, I chose a pink flowery beach dress, thin-strapped and low-necked, a present from my mother for my rare visits to Spain. I'd brought it only because it took up hardly any room and never creased; but somehow it felt right for a summer's evening in the Lakes with a man I barely knew.

Impossible to move in this place without our bodies almost touching. A long awkward moment as I edged past him, avoiding his gaze, using my sponge bag and dress as a shield — then, at last, I was stepping out into the sultry air.

Up in the bathroom, I had a quick shower and combed the tangles out of my hair. The dress fitted like a second skin, and I wondered if it was a wise choice. Too late — Midge was calling me to come to the kitchen when I was ready. Given the layout of the house, there was no chance of me reaching the motorhome undetected to change into something less revealing.

I found the three of them at the table, drinking wine and poring over a spread of takeaway menus. Judging by Jack's raised eyebrows as he sized me up, the dress was *not* a wise choice — but now was not the time for one of my put-downs. Just one more day — then I'd be able to act normally.

As I settled myself on the only spare chair, I couldn't resist giving him a kick under the table. Instantly, with that mischievous glint in his eye, he clamped my leg between his knees.

He handed me a glass of white, his fingers cool against mine. 'That dress you're almost wearing — it's not your usual style. Is it new?'

'No, darling.' A sugary smile. 'I wore it the first time we met — at the ballet. Don't you remember?'

'How could I forget?' He released my leg, thank God, but only to shuffle his chair closer and show me one of the menus. 'We're thinking of eating Chinese. Anything you fancy?'

'Or shall we just pick a few dishes and share them?' Bill put in.

At least that would speed up the process and get Jack away from me. 'Sounds good.'

Midge reached over to the kitchen dresser for a pen and notepad. 'I'll make a list, Bill, if you shout out the numbers.'

'And then you and I are going to collect it,' Jack added, running his fingertip along my arm.

My pulse started to race. 'Don't they deliver?'

'I'd like to show you Keswick.'

I forced a loving look in his direction, and sipped my wine.

Ten minutes later we were on our way, and I decided to turn the unexpected one-on-one time to my advantage. I said evenly, watching for his reaction, 'About your father — it was Bill who mentioned him to me. He assumed I knew the details, and it was quite a challenge to play along.'

His face shuttered. 'How inconvenient for you.'

'Since it's obviously going to come up again, you may as well tell me.'

He was silent for several moments; then, abruptly, 'You like reading the local papers, so you'll find out anyway if you go back far enough.'

I said gently, 'But I need to know now. Later tonight, or tomorrow morning, I'll be discussing you with Bill. Is it really that bad?'

A tightening of his lips, and a haunted look in his eyes that I'd never seen before.

'Jack?' I prompted.

His only response was to turn off the dual carriageway at the next exit. Instead of following the signs for Keswick, however, he took a left towards open country. As we inched along a narrow road in a string of cars, I had more questions on the tip of my tongue. But I held back — vaguely aware that, in his unconventional way, he was about to provide me with some answers.

The silence hung heavy between us, and I turned my attention to the scenery. To our right, flashes of water — one of the lakes we'd seen from the hills — while to our left rose steep wooded crags. Eventually we turned off, and crawled up an even narrower road into another queue of cars. People milled around us — hiking groups, families, couples of all ages. A sudden right turn over a little stone bridge, then into a car park hollowed out of the woodland. Amazingly, someone was just leaving; Jack swung the car into the empty space and we crunched to a halt.

'This is the famous Ashness Bridge. Let's get out.'

'But what about the takeaway?'

'We'll only be a few minutes.'

With a puzzled frown, I did as he suggested.

We threaded our way between the

cars and the crowds, to the stream that gushed under the bridge. He stood on the bank, hands in pockets, head down, while I waited.

At last he spoke. 'I said earlier, there's a time and a place for telling you what happened to my father. This is definitely the place — Barrow Beck, where we scattered his ashes on a winter's day twenty-one years ago.' An intimate confidence that seemed incongruous in such a throng of people, his voice so hushed that I had to lean in to catch his words. But so far I'd heard nothing to explain Bill's astonishment at the Sphinx acquisition. I curbed my impatience; although Jack had chosen the place, it was I who'd dictated the time — and he might need a little longer to prepare himself.

He went on, 'To understand what I feel when I come here, you have to know how he died.' A brusquer tone, as if to keep emotions at bay. 'He worked at Sphinx for over twenty years, and in the end it killed him. Not directly — that happened to two other men, friends of his, an industrial accident that could have been avoided.' His mouth pursed. 'Bad decisions, cost cutting, the usual story of senior managers not doing their job well enough. And, of course, they looked for a scapegoat.' A breath out, long and slow. 'My father took the blame, and then he took his life.'

A stark epitaph; despite the warm evening, I shivered. Jack must have been no more than fifteen when this happened — a difficult age, even under normal circumstances. My thoughts swerved to my own father, a dependable yet remote presence in my mid-teens. Had Dad suffered from any bouts of depression? And would I have noticed if he had? Probably not. Of course, that's what made the impact of suicide so catastrophic for those left behind: the shock and grief at an unexpected death, intensified by incomprehension and guilt.

For once, words failed me. The lonely, lost expression on Jack's face tugged at feelings I usually kept well-hidden. But which role was I playing here? As an executive coach, I'd never had to deal with the fallout from a suicide — or at least not to my knowledge. Outside work, it was the same. In this place, at this moment, with this man, I was out of my comfort zone as a coach — and out of my depth as a girlfriend, real or fake.

And yet . . . it was the girlfriend who prevailed. Even though in this swarm of strangers there was no need for romantic pretence, I put my arms round him and rested my head against his shoulder — an unguarded, unprofessional gesture of compassion. We stood without speaking in this one-sided embrace on the banks of Barrow Beck, while the tourists clattered and chattered past us.

After a while, he disengaged himself and said, his voice cold and clipped, 'So now you can have your next talk with Bill. But otherwise the subject's completely off limits.' Then he spun on his heel and pushed his way back to the parking area, forcing me to grab his arm to stay close.

In the car he wouldn't look at me, concentrating all his attention — it seemed — on manoeuvring his way into the queue of traffic.

I bit my lip. 'Jack, we need to discuss this in more detail. If it's a hidden agenda for the Sphinx acquisition — '

'Who says it is?'

The question hung between us as we edged forward. I stared out of the window, across the bustling bridge to the calm expanse of water beyond. Hours earlier, I'd looked down at the same lake, unaware of this personal tragedy, ignorant of a formative influence on his life. Now the scene was subtly altered: a surface serenity, with deeper undercurrents.

Yet, for whatever reason, he had chosen to bring me here to share the story; I felt strangely privileged.

Sensing his need for space, I made small talk all the way to Keswick; luckily, the traffic had thinned and it took only ten minutes. He drew up outside a cheerful-looking restaurant, its window jumbled with red and gold Chinese lanterns, and turned to me. I saw with relief that his colour was better, his gaze direct once again. 'It'll be busy — do you mind keeping a place in the queue while I park the car?'

Once again I did as he suggested, resisting the temptation to observe that it had already taken us this long — why the sudden hurry? In fact, there was only one other couple waiting; if I'd brought anything to pay with, I could have collected the takeaway while Jack simply drove around the block. Too late now. I explained the situation to the man at the counter, took a seat and thumbed through an ancient copy of *The Keswick Reminder*.

It was a good ten minutes before Jack arrived. 'Took a while to find somewhere to park,' he said, apologetically.

'Really?' I looked pointedly at the pink-and-white-striped bag scrunched up in his hand.

An enigmatic smile. 'Sorry. I had a bit of shopping to do.'

When we were back in the car, he carefully stowed the bag behind his seat, so that I didn't have a chance to speculate on its contents. But whatever he'd bought must have lifted his mood; on the way to Threlkeld he chatted and joked as if the last half hour had never been.

We ate outside again, with the sun setting on the tawny flanks of Blencathra, and Jack's good humour slid predictably into flirtatious banter. At first I played the game reluctantly, my responses dark-edged as I watched the chance of any sort of private conversation with Bill evaporate in the soft evening air. But, as the wine flowed, I came to the realisation that I didn't actually care . . .

And then it was easy to gaze into Jack's eyes from time to time, smile as if I meant it, let his fingers feather my bare shoulder. Like last night, he walked me through the garden; unlike last night, I didn't trip. But, at the carport, on the higher of the two steps up to the motorhome, when he reached past me to open the door, I spun round — and found my face inches from his.

Deep breath. 'Jack . . . I've had such a lovely day, and I . . . I want to say . . . thank you.'

'I've had a lovely day too.' His face was in shadow, eyes unreadable, offering little — if any — encouragement. Even so, flushed with wine — or something less definable — I curled my arms around his neck, and returned the kiss he'd imposed on me, in broad daylight at the top of Skiddaw, as a final proof to Midge that ours was a real relationship.

Except . . . we're in the dark . . . there isn't anyone to convince . . . and it's not a kiss of affection. And you know what? I don't give a damn.

He pulled away, but only after several long seconds; and his hands stayed warm and firm on my waist. Through the flimsy protection of my dress, his touch aroused something instinctive and long-buried. I tilted my head back, but kept my arms where they were, almost in defiance.

'What was that about?' His voice was distant.

I clutched at the nearest straw. 'You kissed me earlier — '

'Not like that . . . *Nothing* like that.'

'Look, it was just a — a natural extension of this evening's role play.'

'Pity you didn't have an audience, then. Even Midge can't see through solid wood, however much she'd like to.' A pause, as he shifted one hand to the nape of my neck, drawing my head closer. 'All the same, maybe we'd better finish what you started.'

My stomach fluttered and my hands fumbled onto his chest, a half-hearted attempt to push him away. 'I think we should — '

Then his mouth covered mine, and I didn't think at all. How could I? All I wanted was to lose myself in the moment, go wherever his kiss would take me, and face the consequences later. Much, much later . . .

When he broke free, when he muttered a good night and walked rapidly away, it was almost a relief. Yet I stood like a statue, until his footsteps faded and I knew he wasn't coming back. Only then did I remember how to move. Slowly, painfully, I switched on the light, gathered up my pyjamas, and stumbled up through the house to the bathroom. Somehow I found my way back to Hermann, built my little wall of cushions and lay down behind it, next to the window.

Why did I kiss him like that? Why did he kiss me back? What the hell have we done?

For what seemed like hours, I watched the moonlight dappling the curtains and willed the tears not to fall.

10

I could still, when I chose, remember so much about that summer with Troy: the glamour of the commonplace when you're in love . . . the intensity of sharing another person's life . . . the waking each morning to a languorous heat. A different heat from the glare outside — the heat of a man's body, half-wrapping mine. The aftermath of making love in the cool of the night.

There'd been a sensuous rhythm to our days together. Each morning I knew that another day was starting, just like the last: a day of being taken to new places — and not all of them points on a map of California. For, in the hands of an expert, I was pursuing a separate journey — one of discovery, desperation, delight. Except that, when you find yourself scaling the heights, you're bound to crash and burn.

And now here I am again, waking to that glorious heat; his limbs heavy on mine, in remembrance of pleasures past, in anticipation of pleasures to come . . .

Still sleepy, I smiled and stretched, wriggled my body further under his and felt him respond, instantly. *Oh yes, my love, breakfast will just have to wait . . .*

Hang on, you're not Troy —

'How in hell's name — ?' I must have uttered it out loud, because he stirred and shifted; but his weight still pinned me to the bed.

'Get *off* me,' I said, shrill with panic, struggling to free myself.

He opened one eye, and his mouth spread into a smile. 'If you ask nicely — '

'Where are all the cushions?' My voice sank to a hoarse whisper. 'What have you done with them?' *It's not really about the bloody cushions, though, is it? It's what they* stand *for . . .*

At last he moved, propping himself up on one elbow and allowing me to breathe more easily; but his lower body stayed where it was. I risked a glance at his bare chest, then lifted my gaze hurriedly to his face.

His brows were drawn together in a frown. 'What have *I* done with them? It was you that started it.'

A sudden chill ran through me. 'What do you mean?'

'You were talking in your sleep, getting upset . . . '

'What was I saying?'

An odd look. 'Nothing I could make out. Why?'

I swallowed. 'And then?'

'You flung the cushions out of the way, and I put my arm round you, and you calmed down.'

'Is that *all*?' I couldn't bring myself to say any more.

He stared at me in narrow-eyed silence, until I couldn't bear it. I looked abruptly away, in the direction of the window, at the sunlight streaming through the thin red curtains. The wood pigeon was back, but this morning its chuntering felt like mockery.

When he spoke, his voice was laced with sarcasm. 'Didn't I say you'd be safe with me — or is your opinion of men so low that you don't believe a word they tell you? Bit of a problem for a coach — maybe you should think of a career change!'

I resisted turning my head; I didn't want to give away the sadness in my eyes, or see the anger in his.

'Alicia.' His voice was soft now, the touch of his fingers on my cheek strangely tentative, yet it told him all he needed to know. 'Why are you crying?'

When I didn't answer, he levered his body up and across so that he was kneeling either side of me. He was wearing boxers, thank God, whereas Troy had always slept naked. But then, all that summer, so had I . . .

Jack's hand cupped my face and pulled it round with gentle force, so that at last I met his searching gaze.

'Why did you kiss me last night?' he said.

'I told you — '

'Tell me the truth.'

Should I? Would it help me to heal — or would it ruin everything? I stared into his waiting blue-green eyes and took the plunge into deep, deep water. 'You accused me of being joyless. Well, believe it or not, this weekend I've remembered what joy feels like. And kissing you was a part of that, as well as a — a way of thanking you.'

'Is crying a part of that, too?' he said, and very carefully brushed my hair away from my damp cheek; an oddly tender gesture that did nothing for my self-control. As I squeezed my eyes shut, he went on, 'He must have been very special, the man who makes you cry.'

'I thought he was at the time, but' — an involuntary dash of bitterness — 'I was wrong.'

'Oh, Alicia.' His sigh was impossible to decipher.

I kept my eyes firmly closed — and also my mouth, which was on the brink of all sorts of betrayal.

He cleared his throat. 'I'm going to have a shower.'

The bed gave up his weight with a groan, and I heard him rummaging for his clothes. When the door slammed, I peeped through my lashes — just in case. But it wasn't a trick; I was all alone, with no one to distract me from my thoughts.

I resolved to make sure there were no more little interludes in the motor-home. Once I was on the train back home, I reasoned, the danger would be over. In the meantime, safety in numbers. I would throw on the trousers and T-shirt I'd worn yesterday and head to the kitchen, in the hope of finding Midge or Bill.

Midge was at the table, sorting through a stack of Sunday papers. 'Morning! Did you sleep well?'

'Very,' I lied.

'Such a pity you can't stay for lunch — Jack says you have a train to catch. But Bill's persuaded him to do a spot of fishing first, so you can have a lazy morning. What time's your train from Manchester?'

I bit back an exclamation; Jack seemed intent on depriving me of a last opportunity to question Bill. 'I'll check my ticket' — another lie, since I could get any train I wanted — 'but it's a real shame we can't stay longer. I've thoroughly enjoyed meeting you.' That at least was true.

'Same here. Still, there'll be other times. Now, help me with these newspapers. Bill takes the finance and business sections when he goes fishing — what do you suggest for Jack?'

'Problem page and obituaries,' I said, waspishly.

A peal of laughter. 'Watch out, Jack — Alicia's got it in for you this morning.'

I whirled round to find him right behind me. Our eyes met; I detected hostility in his, and no doubt he could see the same in mine. But all he said was, 'It's forecast to be another hot day.'

An involuntary glance downwards; he had on the same shorts as yesterday, with a different T-shirt. Less than an hour ago, those legs had been in a far more intimate position . . . I decided to wear shorts too, at least until we were ready to leave; it was time to play him at his own provocative little game.

I turned back to Midge with a bright smile. 'I'll go and get my shower.'

'Mind, you won't see Bill and Jack until later — they'll be off soon, and taking their breakfast with them.'

'Oh.' A pause, while I debated my next step. In a burst of resolve, I spun on my heel, linked my hands around Jack's neck and said huskily, 'Let's make up before you go. You know I can't be angry with you for long.'

I'd hardly finished my sentence when he scooped me up in his arms. 'That's the best offer I've had in a while.' His face was too close, the glint in his eyes too obvious a sign that he was enjoying my look of horror. 'How long have we got, Midge? Don't want to keep Bill waiting, but hey — a man's got to do what a man's got to do.' And, despite my squeals of protest, he carried me out of the kitchen. However much I struggled, he wouldn't put me down. Somehow, he manoeuvred his way up the steps to the motorhome and, finally, deposited me none too gently on the rumpled bed.

'Jack, no!' My voice was sharp with fear; but was it fear of him, or fear of myself?

'Don't worry, this is as far as the role play goes.' A different glint in his eyes now, impossible to fathom. 'And sorry about the fishing, but I didn't feel I could turn Bill down. Anyway, you'll probably get as much out of Midge — if not more.' And, once again, he walked away — leaving me to reflect on what might have been.

Even after my shower, I felt hot and angry. As a farewell gesture to any work agenda, I put on the olive-green shorts I'd brought — skimpy, but cool — and a tight-fitting sleeveless shirt with a sunflower design. My arms and legs looked pale and uninteresting; maybe I'd take some days off next month and sunbathe at my parents' villa. The thought took me by surprise; it was as if I was contemplating a return to normality — or, at least, what I imagined was normality for an unattached twenty-nine-year-old woman.

I found Midge on her own in the kitchen, loading a tray for two: tea, fruit, croissants, jam. She glanced up. 'I thought we'd eat in the garden, there's some nice shade near my studio.'

Intrigued, I followed her along a different path to a sizeable summer house with a table and chairs outside. Only two chairs; evidently a more private retreat than the bigger entertaining space we'd used previously. I peered surreptitiously through the windows of the summer house, but couldn't make much out. In any case, it felt wrong to look without permission.

We sat down and Midge poured the tea. Around us basked the garden, breathing out its scents; the warm breeze ruffling the air seemed to amplify the hum of the bees. The tortoiseshell cat strolled towards us and rubbed affably against my legs.

'Hello, where've you been?' I said, stroking its gleaming amber-and-black fur. 'Haven't seen you since we arrived.' *Which seems a lifetime ago.*

Midge handed me the plate of croissants. 'You're very honoured to see her at all. She's a law unto herself — aren't you, Toffee?'

We both lapsed into a companionable silence, broken only by 'More tea?' or 'Could you pass the fruit, please?'

I feel at peace, for the first time this weekend. Is it because of what's here — the bees, the greenery, the cat? Or is it because of what's not *here — the man who destroyed my equilibrium almost as soon as I met him?*

Eventually, Midge spoke. 'Would you like to have a look round my studio?'

'Yes, please.' I finished the last flakes of my croissant. 'I've seen some of your watercolours already, I'd love to see more.'

She grinned. 'Jack's my best customer, bless him. And he's no mean hand at painting himself, says he finds it therapeutic. Come along.'

It was cooler and quieter inside the summer house. On the walls, in between wide windows, hung several canvases. The rest were stacked around the room — except for one, on an easel in the middle. At first, it was the contents of the walls that absorbed me. Soft hues of green, brown and blue alternating with grey and black and white: the same scenes depicted at different seasons. Accomplished, restful — like the paintings I'd noticed at Leo Components.

I turned to the easel, and stopped dead. As a portrait amongst all the landscapes, it would have stood out anyway. But this wasn't just any portrait. The face, with its wide, wicked smile, took me aback. While the features were now familiar, the sensations they aroused were definitely not. *Not since California* . . .

I lingered, looking my fill, only half aware of Midge beside me.

'Would you like to have it?' She added, with a rueful laugh, 'When it's finished, of course. I'm still trying to get that expression in his eyes right.'

'Looks perfect to me,' I said, absently.

'Not that you need a portrait when you have the real thing.'

'No . . . and the map is not the territory.'

'True.' A pause. 'But, as the years pass, I've found it's important to remember what drew you to a person in the first place. Och, not what they looked like — a photo can do that. Something more elusive. *That's* what I'm trying to catch here.'

I swallowed. 'I think you've succeeded.'

'Thank you. Jack's a difficult man to capture, in more ways than one.'

I moved away from the portrait to the safety of the landscapes, forced some nonchalance into my tone and said, 'Karina doesn't seem to have a problem getting him to come running.'

'Huh, *Karina*. Yes, for years she had him just where she wanted him. One of those relationships where you can't understand why they're together in the first place. Different values, different interests . . . Of course, they had one terrible thing in common — what happened to Jack's father also happened to Karina's.'

I jerked round. 'Oh? I hadn't realised.'

She sighed. 'That's how it all started — isn't a problem shared meant to be a problem halved? But Karina's problems go much further than that, whereas Jack . . . Just take it from me, he's a keeper — is that the right word these days? Anyway, with Karina he knew for a long time it wasn't working, but he couldn't bring himself to break it off — or at least not permanently — because they'd both been through so much already.'

'And then?' I prompted.

'Then he came to his senses and finished it for good. At first she didn't seem to mind, because she had Henrik fawning over her. But then she started hassling Jack. It got so bad that he phoned Bill to ask him what he should do — and guess what my dear husband of twenty-six years suggested?' A throaty chuckle. '"Take out a different girl every night, and make sure Karina — and her crowd — can read all about it. She'll soon cool off — she won't like the competition and her friends will tell her you're not worth it.' So that's why Jack became Jack the Lad.' A pause; then in an anxious voice, 'You do know it was all a pretence, don't you?'

Her words undermined my professionalism in one fell swoop. My local media research had revealed the map, not the territory — and I'd been all too ready to think the worst. I bit my lip and attempted to cover my confusion. 'Why didn't Jack ever bring Karina here?'

An amused glance. 'You've seen her

— can you imagine her tramping up hills? No, by the time we bought this place, Jack was in the process of splitting up with her and bringing her here would have sent entirely the wrong message.' She pulled a face. 'But we've had the pleasure of her company at other times. Now that he's got you, of course, everything's changed.'

'It's just that . . . he says she wants him back, and she's threatening to turn up here this weekend to talk things through.'

'Might be a good idea if she did, Alicia. One look at you and Jack would tell her she's got no hope.' A beady look straight at me. 'There is one thing that bothers me, though.'

I met her gaze carefully. 'Yes?'

'Why would he continue with his dating charade after he met you? Because I know he's been out with other women in the last couple of months, that's why he was never free at weekends to come and see us. I tackled him about it yesterday, on the way up

Skiddaw, but I didn't get a very satisfactory answer.'

That wasn't much to go on; and she was obviously expecting me to elaborate. 'It's . . . complicated,' I said, lamely, and turned away. 'I've got my own baggage to deal with, and the thought of another relationship scares me stiff. I haven't made it easy for Jack — in fact, I haven't made it easy for myself.' I let out a long, slow breath; it was a confession I hadn't intended, but the wave of release felt surprisingly welcome.

There was just one piece of reassurance still required. I went on, 'Do you think he's really over Karina? I mean, I've *seen* the effect she has on him.'

'Believe me, Alicia, you've seen nothing more than his guilt — combined with her growing drink problem.' She glanced at her watch. 'Good grief, is that the time? The men will be back soon, and I want to make you a packed lunch for the journey. Would you like to give me a hand?'

I nodded, grateful for the offer of a distraction from my thoughts. Back in the kitchen, however, the practical tasks and light conversation failed to deliver. Oh, I'd found out all I needed to know about Karina — but what had I achieved? It had merely served to reveal my shortcomings, both professional and personal.

Because I'd jumped to conclusions without establishing the facts, in order to turn Jack Smith into a clone of Troy Randall Travers. Why? Two reasons. First, so that I could punish Jack for everything I'd allowed to fester for the last three years.

And second — to defy the same laws of attraction, and stop myself from being hurt all over again.

11

When the sandwiches were made, I excused myself and went to pack my things, taking the opportunity to write down some of what Midge had told me. Not that I enjoyed facing up to my flaws — although it served as a reminder to contact Judy, one of Coaches for Growth's associates, for some professional supervision.

I'd just finished my notes and was rummaging in my suitcase for the cropped trousers I'd worn yesterday, when Jack came in. I straightened up instantly. 'Very nice,' was all he said, looking me up and down.

My throat felt inexplicably dry. 'Actually, I'm about to take them off.'

'Your legs?'

Nervous giggle. 'No, silly. My shorts. I can't wear these on the train.'

'I don't see why not. They'd certainly

brighten someone's day.'

I flushed, awkward as a teenager. But it was the opening I wanted, and my gaze held steady. 'It's like a replay of our first meeting, isn't it? You eyeing me up and making personal comments. Perhaps, back then, I over-reacted because I bought into your playboy image. But apparently your media campaign was just an act, to put Karina off.' Deep breath. 'I don't know about her, but it had *me* fooled — you were a condemned man as soon as I started my research. Even worse, I brought my prejudices to that first meeting. I owe you an apology, so,' — another deep breath — 'I'm sorry.'

His eyes widened. 'Apology accepted. Some of the things you said and did — they make more sense now.' A rueful laugh. 'Believe it or not, it was quite a challenge to organise a different woman two or three times a week, especially for me.' A flash of that wide, wicked grin. 'I'm more of a rifle than a scatter gun — I like to identify the target, take aim, *then* fire.'

A sudden intensity in the air; I groped

for a way to defuse it. 'Interesting metaphor. Maybe we should explore it at our next coaching session.'

'Why not now?'

'I don't think that's a good idea.'

Maybe my eyes gave him a different message, because he moved closer. The edge of the bed trembled against the back of my knees. I waited — the butterfly on the point of a pin; except . . . No, I couldn't — I wouldn't — play the part of a victim. Not this time.

He said, soberly, 'I know how you kiss when you want to say thank you. I wonder how you kiss when you want to say sorry?'

'Let's find out.' I framed the words, but no sound came. And, in any case, words were redundant . . . We sank as one onto the bed, in a kiss that was startlingly slow and deliberate and tender; yet it wasn't long before it began to build towards something else. We rolled over, mouths still fused, so that his hands could discover unhindered the loosening of my clothes. In an almost leisurely fashion, he reached under my shirt to play with the clasp of my bra, a tease to my growing impatience. Then, at last, he undid the hooks, and his warm fingers skimmed my bare skin to claim my breasts —

The trill of a phone. My phone. My work phone, with its special ring. Just the wake-up call I needed!

He broke off the kiss to say, 'Don't answer it.' It was almost a plea.

But I scrambled off the bed before he could stop me, pulling my shirt down and myself together. 'It's my boss, it must be urgent.'

'Urgent?' His tone sharpened. 'On a Sunday?'

'I'm still working, remember?' It was a reminder to myself as much as to him. I grabbed my phone from the kitchen counter and turned my back on the bed; more of a statement to the man lying there than an attempt to keep the conversation private. 'Yes, Stuart?'

'You sound out of breath, Alicia.

Hope it's not an inconvenient time.'

'Not at all.' *In fact, Stuart, you've just saved my life. What the hell was I thinking, letting Jack Smith hit on me?* I swiftly suppressed the thought that I'd been a willing — no, an *active* — partner.

'Good. I'm leaving for the airport shortly — a week of golf in Portugal, remember? — but I've got a favour to ask. You know that international conference in London next weekend?'

I recalled reading about an inaugural event for some new life coaching organisation or other, a passing reference on our online bulletin board. Life coaching was, of course, a related field to executive coaching; but its focus was more personal and — in my experience, at any rate — its practitioners were less likely to follow a professional code of practice. My mind teetered back three years to that New Age-style course I'd taken in California, the chance meeting on the last day in the Los Angeles County Museum of Art, and all that followed. Because the chance meeting had been with one of the life coaches from the course; and not just any coach, but Troy Randall Travers — the most handsome, the most charismatic and the one who, towards the end of the course, seemed to have eyes only for me. *Oh, definitely more of a rifle than a scatter gun — and I still had the scars to prove it . . .*

'Alicia, are you still there?'

My mind swerved back to the present. 'The conference next weekend — what about it?'

'They've booked Judy for the Saturday, a session about transferring learning from the executive coaching world. Unfortunately, she's just been rushed into hospital with appendicitis — the operation was straightforward enough, but she'll be out of action for a few weeks.' This got my full attention. So much for that reminder I'd just written myself! I would just have to wait until she was better; I certainly wasn't going to bare my soul to any of the other supervisors on Coaches for

Growth's payroll.

Stuart went on, 'So I wondered . . . ' I waited while he floundered towards the inevitable question. He cleared his throat. 'Could you take her place?' A pause; then, his voice squeaky with discomfort, 'Please?'

I considered my answer carefully. It was tempting to refuse — on the basis that he couldn't reasonably expect me to work two weekends in a row. There were several other factors to weigh up, however. For a start, Judy had a reputation for choosing quality over quantity in terms of her speaking engagements, which meant that the conference would be worth attending. And then, even though — given my lack of personal commitments — I was probably the only coach free at such short notice, doing Stuart this favour would give me some extra bargaining power as and when needed. Last but by no means least, being fully occupied next weekend might help me to forget the events of this one.

'All right, I'll do it,' I said at last.

'Can you send me all the details and copy in Celia?' I heard the bed creak behind me; before I could escape, Jack's arms were round me, hands clasped loosely under my breasts. A gesture of solidarity, I sensed, rather than a sexual overture; and all the more powerful for it. Yielding to one last role play, I leaned back against him and continued, 'And forward any notes Judy's given you about her talk — I'll have a look on the shared drive as well, once I'm back in the office tomorrow. Oh, and Stuart?' It was as if I didn't want the call — or the embrace — to end.

'Yes?'

'I hope you have a great time in Portugal. Where are you staying?'

'Near Albufeira — six of us in a villa. Thanks, Alicia, I can't tell you how much I appreciate you bailing me out here. By the way, how's your work going up north — everything on track?'

'Of course.' The lie came easily, but perhaps it was simply another version of the truth, relating to the track of my own coaching journey. Because, in spite of everything, this weekend was allowing me to address one problem — even if it might be giving me another.

'And what about supervision? As Judy's not available, shall I ask Tom to give you a call?'

A half-formed decision crystallised in my mind. 'No need. I'll get Celia to arrange a debrief meeting for when you get back. You, me and Gary,' I added, pressing my mobile even closer to my ear in anticipation of his reply.

'Good idea. Looks like we're getting a new assignment that I'd like you to lead on, so the sooner you hand Leo Components over to Gary, the better.'

'Excellent.' A sudden comprehension that today might be the last time I saw Jack, unless . . . I blinked rapidly — which cleared the mist from my eyes, but did nothing for the lump in my throat. 'See you a week on Monday.'

The call ended but the embrace, thankfully, did not. Maybe I'd underestimated the therapeutic value of being held by a man with no obvious agenda. That had never happened with Troy. Looking back, his agenda had been perfectly obvious; I'd just misinterpreted it as something else.

It was Jack who stepped away, breaking the spell and the silence. 'Are you ready to go?' His voice sounded strained.

'Give me five minutes.' I kept my back to him as I fumbled with the fastening of my bra.

'Here, let me.' His hands took over the task — efficient and deft, with no thought of lingering. Not like before the call. He cleared his throat. 'Why don't you get what you need from your case? Then I can take it to the car while you change.'

Without a word, without even a look, I retrieved my trousers and closed my suitcase. It was easier than expected to busy myself with bed-making until he'd gone. I changed my clothes in slow motion, as if putting off my goodbyes — and not just the ones with Midge and Bill. Finally, I was ready to leave; I twisted the shorts into a tight ball and buried them in my laptop bag. Symbolic, no doubt — but this wasn't the moment for self-analysis.

I could hear the others as soon as I entered the house: a blend of laughter coming from the kitchen, Jack's long and low and instantly recognisable. I paused, welded a smile onto my face, then stepped purposefully through the doorway.

Midge spun round. 'Hi there! We were just planning where to go next time you come — '

'And Jack said he doubted that'd be any time soon,' Bill put in, 'because we'd probably frightened you off.'

'Me especially,' Midge giggled. 'And I told him he was just trying to shame me into some sort of confession about all the dirt I'd dished on him.'

'But I said she was way off the mark,' Jack said, meeting my gaze at last, 'and that it was more about the Hermann effect.'

'The Hermann effect?' I echoed stupidly.

Jack came straight over and put his arm round me, and I realised, with a pang, that this was the final act of our role play. 'You weren't expecting to sleep in a vintage motorhome, were you, love? You like your five-star luxury.'

My smile flickered as I lifted my eyes to his. 'But maybe Hermann has something that money can't buy.' And I felt my cheeks burn as I recalled recent events in the motorhome . . .

Midge was talking; I made a determined effort to concentrate. ' . . . And we'll get the spare room sorted, so you'll be able to sleep there next time. Not that it'll be five-star luxury,' she added hastily, 'but it'll be a lot more comfortable — and much nearer the bathroom, of course.'

I shot a desperate look at Jack, but all he did was tighten his grip on my shoulder. 'Great, we'll look forward to it, although Alicia seems to have a soft spot for Hermann after all.'

We said our goodbyes to Midge and Bill. The warmth of their hugs disconcerted me, but only for a moment; the extraction of my promise to come back soon weighed more heavily on my conscience.

In the car, Jack launched straight into an account of the fishing, while I stared out of the window. I wondered if he was talking about his one-on-one time with Bill to provoke me. Not that I needed reminding how badly I'd neglected the business agenda in favour of a far more personal one. As a result, I had merely the sketchy beginnings of a deep dive, instead of the detailed output I needed for the debrief with Stuart and Gary.

Except . . . it was worth it, in spite of the emotional upheaval. If this weekend — this man — has taught me anything, it's that I'm ready to live my life in colour again, not black and white. It might be the delicate hues of a Midge landscape — that's more my style than a vibrant oil painting — but it won't be the tentative, easily-rubbed-out lines of a pencil drawing. Not any longer. Even if, like last time, I get hurt . . .

For now, though, I had to pull myself together. And, fortunately for me, I suspected that Jack Smith the temporary boyfriend would provide some key insights into Jack Smith the company director. *I'm more of a rifle than a scatter gun — identify the target, take aim*, then *fire*. As I'd said at the time, it was an interesting metaphor. And the demonstration that followed . . . I closed my eyes — to shut it out or re-live it?

'Sorry, Alicia, didn't mean to give you a lecture on trout flies.' His words hinted at a change of subject, and I roused myself for more of a two-way conversation. He went on, 'Call it nerves, I suppose. Because, now that the role play's over, we can go back to normal. Trouble is, I've forgotten what normal feels like.'

'Same here,' I said, without thinking.

'I'm glad about that, I knew it wasn't just me. There's a — a connection between us, on all levels, isn't there? I don't know how else to describe it — maybe you should have a go.'

But I can't, Jack — not while I'm still your coach. Trust me on this — it won't work.

I cleared my throat. 'As I said at our first meeting, coaching requires rapport — '

'But I'm not talking about the coaching.' A pause, while he overtook a dawdling caravan. 'Look, Alicia — right here, right now, we're in between the two sets of roles — aren't we? We'll never get this chance again, and there's so much I have to say to you. Let's spend the rest of the day together!'

Scary to hear that animation — no, excitement — in his voice. Reminds me of the union meeting, when he outlined the new corporate vision. Except then I was impressed, whereas now . . .

He went on, as if oblivious to my silence, 'We've got enough sandwiches to feed an army, or we could go to a pub — my local does a great Sunday lunch. And, of course, I'll take you into Manchester for your train home whenever you want. How does that sound?'

Fraught with danger. Need to put some distance between us, in case I say — or do — something I'll regret. I said, with cool conviction, 'Please drop me at Preston station as soon as possible — I noticed on Friday that it wasn't too far from the motorway. And thanks for the offer of lunch, but I'll eat my sandwiches on the train.'

A pause; then a terse 'Ouch'.

I risked a glance at his face, but its shuttered look told me nothing. I pressed my point home regardless; perhaps it was as much to convince myself. 'We *have* to return to our proper roles, executive coach and coachee — '

'If that's what you think we are.'

'The role play was a means to an end — you said so yourself when we arrived at Threlkeld. From an executive coaching perspective, we've made some progress — just not as much as I was expecting.'

'And from other perspectives?'

'Such as?'

'We made far more progress as a man and a woman.'

'But, as I've said, that was merely a means to an end — '

'If that's what you want to believe.'

I did want to believe it. I had to, even though the memories collected along the way were proving impossible to erase. I lapsed into silence — it was by far the safer option.

After a while he said, 'What happens next?'

I fought back a bitter little laugh; was he talking about us as a coach and coachee, or as a man and a woman? As always, it was easy to pull on my professional mask. 'Well, based on the last few days, I produce a summary of your current reality — '

'My 'current reality'? How the hell would you know anything about that? I don't even understand it myself.'

I continued, as if he hadn't interrupted, 'Then I send it to you for review. Obviously, I would restrict it to the learning that this weekend provided about your business relationships — '

'How can you? For me, it's jumbled up with all the other stuff.'

He was right, of course; except that I couldn't afford to admit it. I said, as calmly as I could, 'Once you've reviewed the summary, we can explore your options and agree which one's best.' *Little do you know — you'll be doing all that with someone else*.

'You make it sound simple.'

I stared out of the window again. 'Simplification is one of the advantages of a structured process.'

'But it's not simple, is it? Not any more. Everything's changed since you kissed me last night . . . ' His voice trailed away.

'Surely you don't think — '

'I don't know what to think, Alicia. All I know is — I'm finding it bloody hard to separate the coach from the girlfriend.'

I sensed him glance swiftly at me, but

I refused to meet his gaze. 'It'll be different when we're back in a business setting.' The sudden patter of rain on the windscreen was a welcome distraction. 'Looks like your warning about the Lakeland weather wasn't in vain. How far is it to Preston?'

'You're sure about Preston?' His voice was flat with disappointment.

'I'll get the train from there, if you don't mind.'

'And if I do mind?'

Deep breath. 'Jack, you're being ridiculous. This is a business contract and you're putting a lot at risk if you think it's anything else.' I forced myself to look at him. 'Role play's a fundamental coaching tool that I've practised for years — '

'Not that sort of role play, I'll bet.' A sardonic laugh. 'Maybe I'm wrong, maybe I'd better give Adam Chesterfield a call in the morning to compare notes. No wonder you came so highly recommended.'

'How dare you even *think* that!' I

managed to bring my trembling indignation under control and salvage a brisk, almost dismissive tone. 'All I'm saying is that the kissing, and everything else, was just a requirement of this particular role play. Let's face it, Jack, we've spent the entire weekend pretending to Midge and Bill that we're romantically involved — and that I can't be your coach for exactly that reason. But in reality it's the complete opposite. I *am* your coach — and that's why we can't be romantically involved, even if we wanted to be. Whichever way you look at it, there's a conflict of interest.'

I watched anxiously as he frowned at the road ahead for several seconds. In the end he said abruptly, 'Sounds like I've got the wrong end of the stick. I'll drop you at Preston, then.' To my relief, he switched on some music, as if to discourage any more discussion.

When he pulled up outside Preston station, my heart started to thump; this was the moment of parting, when words could so easily be overruled by actions. While he went to fetch my suitcase from the boot, I grabbed my bag and darted into the ticket hall, telling myself it was purely to keep dry.

He strode grim-faced through the doorway, the shoulders of his T-shirt flecked with rain, and handed me the suitcase. Our fingers met and, inevitably, I felt the spark.

I blurted out, 'There's a train due.' I had no idea if there was, but I was desperate to get away. 'Thank you for the lift, and I'll be in touch.' I edged towards the barriers.

'Alicia, wait.' He moved closer, and I glanced up at him — wary, almost fearful. 'When will I see you again?'

'I'll email you over the next few days to arrange a meeting.' An evasive reply, designed to buy me time and space. 'And now I'd better go — '

'Just let me give you this.' From the pocket of his shorts, he pulled out a crumpled yet distinctive paper bag: that mysterious purchase he'd made in

Keswick, when we'd been picking up the Chinese takeaway. After the detour to Ashness Bridge, and the revelation about his father. *Was it only yesterday?*

'A souvenir,' he said softly, as he leaned in. 'Of the Lakes.'

'Please don't.' Did I mean the gift, or the kiss? Either way, it was too late. I couldn't stop him from slipping the souvenir into my bag — just as I couldn't stop his arms from enfolding me, and my mouth from opening under his.

He broke off to say, 'Let's go somewhere — anywhere. We need to talk.'

I looked around wildly — a man in railway uniform a few steps away — my brightest smile, as I wrenched myself out of Jack's grasp. 'Excuse me, I've got a ticket for the next train to London — '

'Best come straight through, love,' the man said, instantly. 'You've only got three minutes and those bags'll slow you down.'

He opened the ticket barrier for me, and I stumbled through its jaws. I heard them clamp shut again, and a heated exchange break out behind me. The man was refusing to let Jack follow without seeing his ticket first, thank God — but what if he had time to buy one and catch the same train?

I battled the temptation to look back and dashed to the platform. The train was just pulling in, and I waited impatiently for the door locks to be released. As soon as they opened, I jumped on board, and collapsed into a pair of empty seats halfway along the carriage, straining to listen for any telltale sounds above my gasping breath. No running footsteps, no shout of my name — I was safe.

The train eased away from the station, gathering speed at a relentless rate. But it wasn't until we were past Manchester that I tore my unseeing gaze from the rain-streaked window and fumbled in my bag for Jack's gift. I unwrapped it, carefully, and found a cocoon of white tissue paper. Inside nestled a sturdy painted china figure, only a few inches high.

She was just as I remembered: little black snuffly nose and bright eyes, peeping from under a white cap that barely contained her prickles; starched white apron over a bulky striped petticoat; tiny front paws holding two long, freshly laundered, pale-yellow gloves . . . *No, aren't they some stockings belonging to one of the hens who's always scratching in the farmyard?*

For this was Mrs Tiggy-Winkle, Beatrix Potter's little washerwoman-hedgehog who lived over the back of Catbells . . .

I cradled her in my lap for the rest of the journey and stared out at the blurred world beyond the window. Only when we reached Euston did I realise that the misted view had nothing to do with the rain.

12

I returned to the office with fresh resolve: to spend the week preparing to hand over my coaching assignment, and avoid any calls from Jack — until I was ready.

In fact, it was Wednesday morning before I heard from him; and then, rather than the warmth of his voice, it was the impersonality of an email, sidling into my inbox while I was in a meeting.

The subject line 'Contract Variation' gave nothing away:

> Dear Alicia
> I see from the Coaches for Growth contract (section 11) that I can ask for a different coach.
> I'm sure you'll agree that bringing our relationship to an end is the best way forward. This decision has

nothing to do with your coaching input to date, which has been highly professional and very productive.
Rgds
Jack

I sat in stunned silence. The email bore uncanny similarities to the one I'd been composing in my head, the one I'd planned to send following my meeting next Monday with Stuart and Gary. I should have been delighted that he'd spared me the bother; but it wasn't like that at all. My email would have prefixed the word 'relationship' with 'working' or 'business', whereas his didn't. Which somehow made his message all-encompassing and . . . final. Especially when I recalled his admission from our tense conversation in the car: *I'm finding it bloody hard to separate the coach from the girlfriend*.

Ironic, wasn't it? He was breaking off all contact, just as I was terminating the business relationship in order to become available for something else . . .

'You okay?' Celia slouched into view,

and I hurriedly clicked the email shut.

'Of course,' I said, brightly. Good grief — for *her* to notice, I must have looked even worse than I felt. 'What can I do for you?'

'That conference at the weekend, shall I confirm your room?'

'Room?'

'Judy's got one at the hotel where the conference is, and I'll need to switch it into your name. She was booked in for the Friday and Saturday nights — what about you?'

I opened my diary and found the details of the conference. An informal drinks party on the Friday evening, which I had no intention of attending, followed by a 9 a.m. start the next morning; staying over on Friday was a no-brainer. Saturday's programme kicked off with a keynote speech from a surprise guest, then followed a meandering procession of speakers, breakout groups and panel discussions until the wrap-up at 6 o'clock. The conference would be rounded off with a celebratory dinner. My slot — still badged as Judy, for God's sake! — was towards the end of the day, and I decided that it would be sensible to book the room for a second night; even if I skipped the dinner, the prospect of an evening journey home to an empty flat held little appeal.

'Same,' I said, 'and please make sure there's a bath.'

She seemed about to say something, but didn't — much to my relief.

When she'd gone, I clicked on the email again and re-read his words. How dare he — how *dare* he! The message was clear, and I couldn't help but take it personally: he'd sampled the goods and found them wanting. Perhaps, despite those assurances to the contrary, he'd even gone back to Karina . . .

My lips tightened as I stabbed a reply on the keyboard:

Dear Jack,
I note your request for a different coach, in accordance with section 11 (paragraph 2) of our contract with

Leo Components, and agree that terminating our relationship is the best way forward. Your new coach will make contact next week. This small delay is due to our internal handover processes and I trust it does not inconvenience you.
With kind regards,
Alicia

That should show him. All I had to do now was finish writing up the deep dive, and plan my meeting with Stuart and Gary. In five days' time, it would be over — and I'd never have to see Jack Smith again.

I hit 'send' and got abruptly to my feet. I needed fresh air, a change of scene, a distraction.

Outside, the fountains danced and sparkled in the sun. I leaned against the warm brick wall of the building, and surveyed the lush green of the lawns and shrubs. Everything looked unbelievably bright and clean and *manicured* — when what I longed for were darker colours and rougher edges . . .

One weekend of strange intimacy with Jack Smith — that's all it took to disrupt the bland routine of my existence. Barely two days, in a place of wildness — and I couldn't stop reliving every moment, or fantasising about a different ending entirely. Well, his email had put paid to all *that*.

Later, when I turned the key in the door of my flat, I noted — as if for the first time — the regimented neatness, the sterile atmosphere, the seeming absence of human interaction. Except that, since Sunday night, there'd been a small but important lapse, a surrender to sentiment. On my bedside table stood Mrs Tiggy-Winkle, a symbol of all that had gone right with my weekend in the Lakes — until today. Now she was a reminder of all that had gone wrong.

I went into the bedroom and placed her resolutely in the drawer below; out of sight, out of mind.

If only it was that simple. The next

two days were spent with the spectre of Jack Smith as I completed the deep-dive report based on all the information I'd gathered. It was a work of art, crafted from personal as well as professional observation, but carefully worded to cover up any visible cracks in my coaching armour. And yet . . . every comment was weighed down with memories and double meaning. 'Jack is quick to take the initiative and responsive to feedback. This was apparent following the senior management meeting and subsequent debrief, when he researched more consultative leadership techniques and implemented them at the union meeting the next day.' *Even more apparent on the Saturday night, when I kissed him and he gave back as good as he got . . .* 'He can be very persuasive and single-minded in pursuing his own agenda. He volunteered the metaphor of a rifle shot — identify the target, take aim, then fire.' *A metaphor that we started to explore together, in a motorhome called Hermann, until we were interrupted by a phone call . . .* 'He seems to be widely respected by the workforce because, as one of the union representatives explained, he's given them hope.' *And that's exactly what he gave me — hope of finding love again. This time with somebody more capable of returning it. And now that hope's been well and truly dashed . . .*

Every so often, by way of light relief from the deep dive report, I reviewed Judy's notes on the session she'd been going to deliver at the conference. She made transferring the learning from executive coaching to life coaching sound straightforward, a matter of imposing structure and formality. The irony of being her replacement wasn't lost on me: these notes would be delivered by a woman who'd apparently learnt very little from her career as an executive coach. A woman who'd just allowed a disastrous personal event from her past to screw up a client relationship. Even worse, a woman who'd been on the brink of falling in love with that same client . . .

Friday evening drifted up on me like a mist. As I intended to go straight into London from the office, I worked late. Not that I had much actual work to do by then; it was more a case of filling in time until I could be sure of avoiding any involvement with the informal drinks party.

To my surprise, Celia was at her most helpful, staying beyond five o'clock and offering to book me a taxi to the station. Bemused, I allowed her to organise my journey and arrived at the hotel around eight. True enough, my room had a bath — and not just an apology for one. I turned on the taps, reckoning that it would take a while to fill the deep tub with enough water for a relaxing soak. In the bedroom I unpacked and undressed, eking out both tasks with the expertise of someone used to long hours of solitude. Then it was on with the sleek white velour robe provided, and on with the kettle.

Good selection of tea — too much

choice, in fact. Peppermint? Earl Grey? Or maybe —

A knock at the door. Room service, confusing me with another guest? I let out an exasperated sigh, tightened the belt of my robe and crossed the room. The security chain meant that the door opened no more than a couple of inches — wide enough to send whoever it was away.

'Yes?' My tone was designed to give the shadowy figure standing in the corridor no encouragement. Judging by the height, this must be a man; the subdued glow of the corridor lighting hampered any further identification.

'It's me, Alicia.'

That unmistakable black-velvet voice — its simple, intimate greeting directed at *me*. I stared in disbelief, waiting for this weird dream to relax its grip. But no — as my eyes adjusted to the half-gloom, I could make out everything that was now familiar about Jack Smith: the shape of his head, the cut of his shoulders, the angles of his face

. . . The drab remains of the evening took on a new lustre — and this moment was something to savour, rather than rush. 'What are *you* doing here?' I managed, at last.

The ghost of a grin. 'That very much depends on you.'

'In what way?' My gaze lingered on his mouth, while my mind battled those inevitable memories.

'I thought we could have that talk, the one we didn't have on Sunday.' A pause, while he looked me up and down. 'I was going to suggest we went to the bar — '

'Let's stay here,' I said firmly, undoing the security chain; the last thing I wanted was to be in the company of others when we talked. Yet, as he came through the door, I found myself turning away in confusion. No need for role play any more — but would our script have changed?

I blurted out the first thing that came into my head. 'I was just making tea — would you like some?'

He cleared his throat. 'Got anything stronger?'

'You'll have to make do with strong tea,' I said primly, recovering my composure. 'Sit down.' I gestured to the easy chair furthest from the bed, and busied myself with taking two teabags out of their sachets.

A low chuckle. 'I love it when you boss me about.'

An invitation to give him other orders, like 'Hold me' and 'Kiss me' and 'Take me to bed'? But I said nothing. Meanwhile, on its little wooden shelf, the kettle grumbled loud and long, erupted into a crescendo of boiling, and came to rest. I poured the water into the chunky china teapot, and set out the two cups and saucers. With the kettle silenced, there was nothing to drown out another sound — the sound of running water . . .

I dashed into the bathroom and turned off the taps, not a moment too soon. My heart was thumping, and it wasn't just because of the near-flood. I knew he was behind me, and I knew what would happen next. My fingers fumbled with the belt of my bathrobe, then stopped. Why deprive him of the pleasure?

'Alicia.'

I turned, as if in slow motion; our eyes met and held. In the end, it was my voice that whispered the question: 'Do you want to talk now . . . or later?' He gave me his answer without uttering a single word, untying my bathrobe, easing it from my shoulders, letting it slide to the floor. Then he stepped away, undoing the buttons of his shirt, studying every inch of me through half-lidded eyes. My initial embarrassment at his scrutiny soon gave way to impatience, and I moved nearer to help him off with his clothes. When at last that was done, I could admire — more openly than ever before — the taut, lean beauty of his body.

And so we resumed what had begun in the motorhome — a journey into the known and the unknown, the familiar and the new, the anticipated and the unexpected. With it — for me, at least — came the erosion of old barriers, the healing of secret hurts, the rediscovery of the very essence of living.

We made love slowly, wonderingly, joyfully. The tea cooled in the teapot, the water lay undisturbed in the bath. And, after three long years, the ice that had numbed my heart began to thaw.

13

I awoke to sunlight framing the dark panel of the curtains, and to the heat of Jack's legs entwined with mine; I lay for a while, basking in the lingering warmth of the night's recollections. Then I turned my head towards him and noted — as I'd done once before — the way that his hair stuck up at the front. I was just reaching out to smooth it, when he opened his eyes.

That smile — wide, wicked and beloved — lit up his face. 'Pinch me, I'm dreaming.' When I obliged, he responded with an exaggerated howl of pain. Then, pretending to scold, 'You'll have to be punished for that.'

'But I was only doing what you — ' His mouth blotted out my words, while his hand followed a teasing trail down my body. Oh . . . if, during the act of love, deferred gratification can be considered exquisite torture — then what followed was certainly a form of punishment.

A long time later, I glanced at the clock and sat bolt upright. Eleven forty — wasn't I meant to be somewhere? Ah yes, there was a conference going on. Since I'd already missed most of the morning sessions, I decided to wait until the programme re-started at two o'clock. If I wasn't due to speak until half past three, it would give me an opportunity to acclimatise. It would also give me time for a leisurely lunch beforehand, with the man lying beside me.

Funny how standing in for Judy at the conference had turned from job ammunition into an inconvenience. As if reading my thoughts, Jack laced his fingers through mine and said softly, 'Do you really have to go?'

I sighed away my regrets. 'Yes, but not yet. Fancy something to eat?'

'You know me, the way to my heart is through my — ' He stopped, and gave a low chuckle. 'Actually, there are two ways to my heart and you know both of them.'

'Mmm.' I smiled as I thought of the memories we'd been building. 'But not as well as I'd like to.'

'Sounds like I'll need a nap this afternoon, to gather my strength for tonight.' He lifted our joined hands briefly to his lips. 'Shall I book somewhere for dinner?'

'That would be lovely. For lunch, we can just get a sandwich.'

'Or two,' he added, grinning.

In the event, it was three, and they were quite substantial; we shared them under the trees in a nearby park. Predictably, he ate more than I did — and, just as predictably, we got covered in the newly mown grass. Not that it mattered; after showering earlier, we'd just thrown on what we'd worn yesterday. I had a different outfit in mind for the conference, and he was planning to buy a change of clothes.

'Get yourself a razor, too,' I reminded

him, running a finger across his chin. 'It's like kissing Mrs Tiggy-Winkle.'

He laughed. 'Did you like your souvenir of the Lakes?'

'Loved it.' A pang of conscience as I remembered where I'd put it. 'You know, you're far nicer than I gave you credit for earlier in the week.'

His eyes held mine in a searching look. 'You know why I sent that email?'

'I think I do now, although I didn't realise at the time.' Another pang as I recalled how, driven by self-preservation, I'd assumed he was giving me the brush-off.

'I had to end our business relationship so that *this* could happen. Because I want — I need a different relationship with you, and more than a physical one. Not that I'm complaining,' he added, linking my hand with his.

'You certainly weren't complaining last night — or this morning.' I settled myself in the crook of his shoulder; being away from the bedroom was certainly more conducive to talking. 'But I wasn't expecting to see you at all, ever again. I took your email as a 'thanks, but no thanks' — to the girlfriend as well as the coach.'

'What the — ?' He recovered himself and went on, with a rueful chuckle, 'I chose my words carefully — for once! — because I didn't know if your colleagues would read it. And I thought your snotty little reply was for the same reason — to put everyone else off the scent.'

'Snotty little reply?' I gave him a dig with my elbow. 'It was a masterpiece of restraint, compared with what I wanted to say — and do — to you.'

'Mmm, that could be fun,' — a playful nip at my ear — 'we'd better explore it in our next . . . session.'

A pleasurable pause, while I allowed my mind to wander. 'Don't make promises when you don't know the ask,' I said, at last. 'But there's something else you need to explain. If this trip to London was planned, why didn't you pack a bag?'

He pressed his lips to my hair for a moment, then let out a sigh. 'I kept bottling out, because I still wasn't sure whether I'd got the wrong end of the stick. By Friday, I knew I'd have to do it on the spur of the moment, so I just went straight from the office to the station. Crazy, really, when I'd been thinking about it all week . . . Although in fact I didn't make any definite plans until the Wednesday — Celia was very helpful, as always.'

'*Celia?*' I twisted to face him, wide-eyed. 'You mean she knew you were coming to London?' He nodded. 'That explains a lot,' I went on. 'Her unusual interest in doing her job, for a start. And how you knew exactly where to find me.'

'Don't give her a hard time over it, poor kid.'

'If anyone's going to get a hard time, it'll be you,' I said, with mock severity.

'Don't make promises when you don't know the ask,' he said, teasingly; and he folded me in his arms, making me breathless and grass-stained all over again.

Back at the hotel, I freshened up and slipped into a pair of fitted stone-coloured trousers and my sunflower top. Too formal for a laid-back life-coaching crowd? Definitely. So I left my hair loose instead of in the usual French plait, and brushed it until it shone.

'Beautiful.'

I spun round, relishing the admiration in his voice and in his eyes. He was standing close enough to touch and, since last night, I could reach out and touch whenever I wanted. I said wryly, 'That's reassuring. At least if I mess up my talk, I'll look good doing it.'

He tilted my face towards his. 'Why would you mess it up?'

'Lots of reasons. It's someone else's talk and I'm not as comfortable with the subject matter. I haven't done my usual preparation on the audience, or the venue, or the other speakers — which makes me even more nervous.

And, most of all, I just want to be here with you.'

'Take this as a souvenir.' He bent his head and kissed me. 'What time do you think you'll be finished?'

'I'll leave as soon as the panel discussion's over — shouldn't be any later than five. You'll be back from your shopping trip by then? There's only the one key card.'

'I'll be here waiting for you, Alicia.'

I gave a ragged sigh. 'Look, if I don't go this very second, I won't go at all.'

'Let's go together, then, and I'll get my shopping out of the way. Deal?'

'Deal.'

Downstairs, in the crowded lobby, we parted with nothing more than a lingering look and a touch of the hand. I watched his retreating back until he disappeared from view. Then I squared my shoulders and followed the signs for 'Aspire and Inspire: International Life Coaching Conference'.

A printed name badge lay in splendid isolation on the registration table;

needless to say, it was for Judy. I waited, serene and unquestioning, while one of the organisers corrected it with a handwritten label. Somehow, this persistent refusal to accept me as a replacement no longer mattered. In fact — I smiled to myself — maybe it was a sign that I wasn't meant to be here at all, that I should've gone shopping with Jack.

I was shown to a seat on the low stage, one of five in a shallow semi-circle. To my left — a blond man wearing jeans, sandals and a startlingly black beard; I judged him to be around Jack's age, and he introduced himself as Lionel. On my far right — two women. Di, the one nearer to me, was perhaps in her late thirties; pretty, with long flowing hair and a long flowing skirt. The one further away, Wanda, looked older and more formal. Her hair was scrunched into a tight little bun that gave her rather a severe air; I was glad I'd left mine loose.

The seat next to mine, the centre of

the group, was empty. I was about to ask who we were waiting for, when the announcer — a large, untidy woman whose bracelets jangled without any apparent effort on her part — summoned Wanda to the middle of the stage as the first speaker. Lionel went next, and then Di. I listened to them in my new frame of mind, benevolent to all. Especially Di, who interspersed her basic message of 'oneness' with whale music and meditation. Instead of contemplating a deserted beach scene, however, I let my mind drift to Jack . . .

Finally it was my turn. I kept to Judy's notes, which I knew more or less by heart. Using anonymised case studies, I explained that, whereas in life coaching the client was an individual, executive coaching was different: the contract was with an organisation and the people being coached were usually its senior managers. As with life coaching, the reason for the intervention was often some sort of change or transition. However, contracting with an organisation introduced a greater emphasis on formality and professional standards, which could help avoid some basic pitfalls.

The audience seemed unimpressed; no doubt the style of coaching I'd described was far removed from what they were used to. So far removed, in fact, that a lecture on the art of vegetable sculpting would probably have been greeted with more enthusiasm. As I surveyed the room one last time, I saw a man at the back step forward, clapping more loudly than anyone else. My heart lurched. It was Jack, in a new checked shirt and chinos, looking ridiculously handsome and proud and — and *happy*. I couldn't resist giving him a beaming smile and a thumbs-up.

One last session — then I could go to him. Dinner, followed by a stroll through the London streets, back to the hotel. Perhaps a nightcap in the bar, delaying the inevitable. Finally, when we couldn't hold off any longer, we would go to bed. I glanced at my watch. Only four or five hours to wait. Unless, of course, there was time before dinner . . .

I had hesitated a moment too long. Now the announcer was between me and my seat, introducing the panel discussion. We would be joined by the keynote speaker, one of the morning sessions that I'd missed. A man who'd apparently held everyone spellbound with a mantra that captured the very essence of our conference title 'Aspire and Inspire': *to be better at life coaching, you have to be better at life*.

I raised my eyebrows; a snappy slogan — but what did it actually mean? My immediate conclusion was that it promoted the very opposite of professional detachment, which was the mainstay of executive coaching. An interesting approach that could provoke a more intense debate . . . Maybe the next hour would be time well spent after all.

'And here he is,' the announcer continued, her tone exultant, 'from the

Golden State of the USA, with his unique brand of coaching wisdom, please welcome once again Troy — Randall — Travers!'

Somewhere inside my head, a drum started its throbbing beat. My face froze in a grimace of shock and confusion. In the midst of thunderous applause, I found myself trapped in an embrace that had once meant more than anything else in the world.

'Aleesha.' A voice not heard for three years — but never forgotten — caressed my ear. 'What an unexpected pleasure! At least, it's a pleasure for me. Let's hope you can say the same.'

14

'Troy — I love your mantra, and what a fabulous session you did this morning. In case anyone here missed it, could you remind us what your style of life coaching involves?'

Was it Wanda or Di who'd simpered the question at the man now sitting to my right? And how in God's name had I reached my seat without passing out? Maybe I *had* passed out, and this was merely a nightmare from which I could awake at any time.

'Hey, Wanda, I'm truly touched — thank you.' He spread his hands — elegant, compelling hands that had once been as familiar to me as the sun and the moon. 'Okay, so whenever I coach someone, I like to be a big part of their life, I call it total immersion. And together we push their boundaries, right? That leads to some amazing experiences — for me as well as the coachee. There's always a confidentiality agreement involved, so I can't be too specific — but let me tell you about a time when . . . '

As he spoke, I forced myself to stop trembling and look at him. He was still, to the unjaundiced eye, powerfully attractive with his flawless tan, youthful face, perfect smile. All testament to the scale of his disposable income; or rather that of Maria, his long-term partner — the woman I hadn't even known about until she returned unexpectedly early from her two-month trip to Europe, tracked him down, and gave him an ultimatum . . .

I'd been haunted by that chapter of my life for three years — until last night. What I'd found with Jack had helped me towards closure. Except now, it seemed, there was one final page to be written — with the man beside me. I drank in every detail, observing the changes: his ever-so-slightly sagging jaw, the puckered skin of his neck

— hints of an old age that could no longer be held at bay. Then my gaze lurched to his hands, and the trembling started all over again.

As if still attuned to my every thought, he paused in the middle of whatever he was saying and said, 'But maybe you should ask Aleesha. As a former coachee of mine, she has first-hand knowledge.'

Somebody laughed; it was a harsh laugh and I realised that it came from me. Because this suggestion was nothing more than a test: as he'd already indicated, the Troy Randall Travers style of life coaching required the coachee to sign a non-disclosure agreement.

And all the time Jack must be watching, and thinking — what *was* he thinking?

Try to breathe . . . swallow . . . take control.

'Alicia?' This was Lionel, concern battling with curiosity in his voice.

I took a gulp of air and dragged my

eyes towards Troy's. 'That's correct. It was a very . . . formative experience that ultimately helped me to decide on a career in executive coaching — '

He pounced. 'Odd decision, when you responded so well to total immersion. Care to elaborate?'

I shook my head. 'As you know, I'm legally bound not to divulge any details.'

A flash of excessively white teeth. 'So am I. All I'll say is — what a waste!' He dismissed me with an exaggerated shrug, and turned to the audience. 'Hey, guys — even if you haven't any direct experience of executive coaching, I'm sure you can imagine how it goes: you sit in an office talking to a manager in a suit about how they're gonna achieve their performance targets, with all the really interesting stuff strictly off limits. What does life coaching need to learn from *that*?'

A crescendo of laughter from the audience and, on the stage, from Wanda and Di — all seduced by his charisma.

Only Lionel and I, it seemed, saw nothing funny in his remarks. Oh, and Jack too; I glimpsed him at the back of the room — arms crossed, face like stone. If it hadn't been for a need to prove myself to *him*, I would have given up there and then.

But actually, it wasn't just for Jack. There was also something inside of me that rebelled at being written off by Troy Randall Travers in such a cavalier fashion; a welling of professional and personal pride that needed to find release.

'That's exactly what I'm here to explain,' I said coolly, once the laughter had died down. 'First, let's look at some similarities. Executive coaching has the same purpose as life coaching — it's just that the life in question is that of an organisation, rather than an individual. And I'm sure you can all appreciate that an organisation still has aims, still needs to deal with change. Which means that, yes, I often sit in an office talking to a manager in a suit.'

I shifted into a more comfortable position on my chair, then went on, 'But that can involve 'really interesting stuff' too. Because, with every coaching assignment, there's an element of unpredictability.' My voice faltered as I recalled that first meeting with Jack at Leo Components; I dragged myself together. 'As for being in an office — well, increasingly, executive coaches are varying the environment in which they work. In fact, this time last weekend I was in the Lake District with my coachee — which helped us both to see things differently.' A quick smile in Jack's direction — seeking a response, but not lingering for one; I needed to focus on Troy.

I turned my head and met his gaze full on. His eyes were blue, like Jack's, but without the green flecks; in fact, there was nothing to disturb their uniformity. How many times had I teasingly compared them to the Pacific Ocean . . . I bit my lip, rousing myself from an old spell. 'To answer your question, however, there is something that the less' — I was tempted to say 'scrupulous', but I resisted — 'less structured forms of life coaching could learn from executive coaching.'

He addressed the audience, mouth sketching an incredulous grin. 'Boy, this is gonna be worth hearing.' Then he switched back to me, almost casual in his confidence. 'Well, Aleesha, what could *I* learn from *you*?'

'Professional ethics.'

The grin flickered. 'Meaning?'

'As we all know, some elements — accreditation, certification, compliance with data protection laws — are relatively straightforward to acquire. But what about the values-based ethics, the principles of honesty, integrity, transparency? What about the duty of care that every coach has — or should have — for their coachee? Talking purely hypothetically, let's suppose that what starts out as a coaching relationship becomes far more personal. Is that professional? Is that ethical? Where are the boundaries?'

The grin widened again, as if he was comfortable with the challenge. 'In my style of life coaching, it's the particular needs of the coachee that determine the boundaries. And then we push them, overcome them. That's the whole freaking idea, Aleesha.'

Titters from the audience, but not the same wholehearted laughter as before; I pressed my point. 'But where does morality come into it?'

'Morality?'

'Suppose your coachee wants to commit a crime — rob a bank, say, or murder their partner. Do you help to remove the boundaries so that the coachee can achieve their goal?'

'That's a ridiculous scenario, I would never take on anyone like that. If you remember, I arrange an initial interview to talk through the coaching assignment, and it goes ahead only if we both agree.'

Oh yes, I remembered. The charismatic coach invited the starstruck student to dinner; a Peruvian restaurant, the conversation as spicily seductive as the food. By the end of the meal, the student believed she needed life coaching to 'find herself'; for an unexpectedly affordable fee, she would have the Troy Randall Travers total immersion experience, his undivided attention for the next two months. Naturally, she 'found herself' — and a lot more besides.

Maybe I was the exception . . . but, based on my recollection of Maria's shrill accusations, I doubted it.

Deep breath. 'Let's take a less ridiculous scenario, then. Suppose your coachee falls in love with you and a different relationship becomes possible. Would you take advantage?'

He reached out and rested his fingers lightly on my bare arm. Only he and I knew that, underneath, his thumbnail was digging into my flesh. I held his gaze, daring him to lie.

'Honey, if I had to count the number of girls who've thrown themselves at me over the years, I'd be here all week.'

He addressed the audience with a self-deprecating grimace. 'As I always say to a female coachee — when it comes to coaching, does it matter whether I'm a man and you're a woman? Unfortunately, to some of them, it does.' Back to me, releasing my arm with an affectionate-looking squeeze. 'With me, people buy the whole package, risks and all, right? The whole point of my total immersion approach is that no one knows how it'll play out.' A laugh devoid of any amusement. 'Not even me.'

It was tempting to reveal the red mark on the underside of my arm, and gain some sympathy votes. But I wanted to win the conversational jousting on level terms.

I forced some lightness into my voice. 'That's no excuse, though, surely? Yes, this girl — these girls should have known better. But it's not an equal relationship, is it? You're the one in charge of the situation, and your role carries some responsibility for their welfare.'

He flung his hands wide, simulating

incomprehension. 'Role? Responsibility? Welfare? Typical corporate crap.' A winning smile at the audience. 'Okay, so let me tell you all about a *really* interesting guy I coached, movie actor — no names, no pack-drill. You'd think this guy would have everything he ever wanted, but . . . '

And on he went, skillfully weaving into his celebrity success story the suggestion that he coached males as frequently as females. Oh, and implying that my reference to professional ethics was an insult to the intelligence.

It was Lionel who hauled him back to my earlier question. 'That's all well and good for a famous film actor, Troy — they probably involve a team of people in everything they do, a readymade support network. But what safeguards do you have in place for everyone else? I suppose with executive coaching, Alicia, the coachee can always refer back to the HR department — is that right?' I nodded. He hesitated, then went on, 'But with life coaching the coachee's on their own.'

Troy's eyes were slits of steel in a bronze mask. 'So's the coach.'

'Don't you have supervision?' This from Di, leaning forward. Not to criticise, of course; more with barely suppressed eagerness — eagerness to learn from the master . . .

He turned to her with a suave laugh. 'I've never found it that effective, but maybe I just haven't found the right person. I'm open to offers, though.' His voice dropped to a husky, intimate tone for these last words, as if there was no one else in the room. I could imagine how it made Di feel — I'd have felt the same. I *had* felt the same, once.

I stared over at Jack, willing him to meet my gaze; but he was looking down at the floor. I switched my attention reluctantly back to Wanda, who was entering the discussion for the first time.

'I don't understand the issue here,' she was saying, her wide forehead creased in a frown. 'We have contracts in life coaching just like you do in executive coaching. It's just common sense to have something in writing explaining each party's responsibilities.'

'Except that the map is not the territory.' The words came automatically to mind, and I spoke them as loudly and distinctly as I could.

Instantly, Troy's head swiveled in my direction. 'What are you talking about?' His tone, to one who knew him well, was subtly threatening; but for me there was no turning back.

Deep breath. 'In the Los Angeles County Museum of Art on Wilshire Boulevard, there's a painting by Magritte, 'The Treachery of Images'. You know it very well, you introduced me to it. A picture of a pipe, with the caption 'This is not a pipe' — '

'In French, of course,' he put in, smoothly. ''Ceci n'est pas une pipe.' And the painting is actually called 'La Trahison des images'.' I suppressed a shiver. His accent was still impeccable; back then, it had added to his allure

— as I was sure it did now, for women like Di. His mouth twisted in a smile, falsely encouraging. 'Your point, Aleesha?'

'A contract, or a non-disclosure agreement, is simply a piece of paper signed without any real understanding of what the coaching experience will involve. The map is not the territory.' I looked carefully past Troy, at Wanda. 'We all know that coaching is an unregulated industry — the executive side just as much as the life side. But a corporate contract is more comprehensive, the coaching is overseen by HR and the coach has their own independent supervisor — which at least gives everyone some protection.' I paused, before allowing my gaze to drift back to Troy. 'Whereas life coaching can take the coachee into treacherous waters, without any obvious way back to safety.'

He manufactured a weary sigh. 'Any coachee can get out of their depth, especially if they're young and deluded. And the skill of the coach is often about communicating the stuff they don't wanna hear. But hey, Aleesha, as an executive coach — and presumably one of the less experienced ones, given your age — have you never found yourself in an inappropriate situation with a client?'

I should have seen the question coming. A few weeks ago, my answer would have been an unthinking 'No' — but now . . .

Caught off guard, I fumbled for the right words, painfully aware that Jack would be listening. 'If there's a — a problem between coach and coachee, then it's usually resolved via a substitution clause in the contract.' I swallowed, and hurried on. 'As I've already said, with executive coaching the focus is more on the organisation's needs, and less on those of the individual being coached. But there is overlap, naturally.' I clutched wildly at an illustration. 'Take a company acquisition: what if the director I'm coaching has personal baggage with the acquired company — something that could cloud their judgement, become a barrier to their performance? As an executive coach, I would want to explore that, up to a point. Unless it requires a different skill set, of course, such as counselling.'

I had Jack in mind, of course — his father's tragic end at Sphinx Industries — but I wasn't referring to him specifically. And yet a sixth sense told me I'd overstepped the mark and handled a delicate subject unprofessionally. I glanced over at him, apologetic smile at the ready; to my dismay, he was halfway out of the room.

I fought the urge to follow him, and stumbled on. 'As I've said, the scope of executive coaching means that problems between coach and coachee are relatively rare and more easily addressed — '

'But, as *I've* said, that same scope means that the really interesting stuff is off limits.' Troy turned to the audience, spreading his hands — an expansive, clever gesture conveying a potent blend of sincerity, humility and passion. 'Remember the mantra? *To be better at life coaching, you have to be better at life*. My total immersion approach offers the widest possible scope — the limits are decided by the coachee's individual needs. As a result, I've experienced life in its widest variety.' He brought his hands together in a parody of prayer. 'Give me life coaching any day . . . the freedom to help another human being identify and overcome their most crippling issues . . . the privilege of knowing that I'm making a real difference to someone's future.' A soft, disarming sigh, as he rested his hands on his knees. 'Okay, so maybe it's because I'm just a simple guy from California, but all that really *matters* to me. The person is more important than the task — every time.'

Impressive performance. Out of the corner of my eye, I saw the announcer glance at her watch and get to her feet. I had one last opportunity to make an impact.

Another deep breath; then, weighing my words carefully, 'I still think that some of the structure and rigour of executive coaching would be beneficial for your approach, Troy.' A minor achievement, saying his name out loud. 'After all, total immersion without a lifeline can end in drowning.'

He said, staring straight ahead, 'Thanks for your concern, Aleesha, but I'm an expert swimmer.'

'I was thinking more about the people you coach.'

A murmur rippled through the audience — condemnation, or approval? Not that I cared — my work here was over. Now I needed to find Jack.

' . . . very stimulating debate,' the announcer was saying. 'Let's have a comfort break before our final session — back here in ten minutes.'

I jumped up instantly. I would go straight to the room, where Jack would be waiting —

'Alicia!' This was Lionel — to my relief; I'd been half-expecting, 'Aleesha!'

I stopped and turned to him. 'Yes?'

'Good discussion back there. Not easy to argue against God's gift.'

A faint smile. 'Thanks.'

'Are you staying for the dinner later?'

'I've got other plans.'

'Oh.' His voice flattened. 'Nice meeting you.'

'And you.'

I spun round, and found myself face to face with Troy; I managed a hasty step back to avoid cannoning into him.

'Be careful, Aleesha.' His hands gripped my upper arms, as if to steady me.

'Oh, I *am*, believe me,' I said, sweetly. 'I've had three long years of practice at being careful.' Until last night, of course. Last night, I had abandoned my carefulness and discovered something beautiful, and right, and shared.

I jerked my arms free, banking on the fact that Troy wouldn't cause a scene in public. As I marched away, I was vaguely aware of Di moving in, preventing him from following. I felt a surge of gratitude, mingled with pity.

'Alicia, wait!' Wanda's voice, just as I was nearing Reception.

I stopped and turned, covering my

frustration with a polite smile. 'Yes?'

She herded me to one side. 'I just wanted to thank you.'

'Oh — what for?'

'Put it this way — when I listened to Troy this morning, I was a convert. Now I've changed my mind. It was when you said 'the map is not the territory' . . . I thought, yes — how can the coachee know what they're letting themselves in for? I mean, that's true of any sort of coaching, but especially this total immersion of his. And if he doesn't feel any responsibility . . . ' She shuddered.

'I appreciate you telling me this, Wanda.'

'Aren't you coming to the next session?'

'Sorry, I've got to make an urgent call.'

'Okay, maybe we can catch up later.'

I nodded brightly and edged towards the staircase — better than waiting for the lift and risking another interruption. Up I went, two stairs at a time, and reached the room at last, a breathless apology on my lips. But there was no answer to my knock. No Jack — not even a stone-faced one — coming to let me in. Maybe he was having that nap he'd mentioned. I would need to get another key card . . .

Back down the stairs to Reception, rehearsing my request: *Have you a spare key card for room 109? My boyfriend's fallen asleep.*

When at last I blurted this out to the man behind the desk, he looked at me in surprise. 'Your key card's here, your boyfriend handed it in when he left.'

Stay calm . . . deep breath. 'Did he say how long he'd be?'

The man pursed his lips. 'Sorry, no message.'

'When did he go out?'

'Five minutes ago, maybe ten. No more than that.'

If I hadn't been delayed, I'd have seen him . . . I blinked several times to clear the sudden mist from my eyes. 'The key card, please.'

'Certainly, here it is.'

This time I climbed the stairs at a

more measured pace, willing myself to believe — oh, all sorts of things. That he'd gone out on a last-minute errand — the razor that I'd teased him about, perhaps . . . That there'd been a misunderstanding about meeting in the room, and he was waiting for me in the bar . . . Or, most likely, the man at Reception was an incompetent fool and had confused Jack with someone else — which meant that this was a spare key card after all, and Jack simply hadn't heard my knock.

And then . . . as soon as I opened the door of room 109, I knew that he wasn't there. I stood on the threshold and let the emptiness sink in. He'd made the bed before he left — not very proficiently, as though in a hurry. But was it a hurry to get his errand over and done with, or a hurry to be away before I returned? I would know soon enough. No sign of his clothes, the ones he'd been wearing before he went shopping. In fact, I couldn't see any trace of him . . . Except for a piece of paper next to the kettle, starkly white against the dark wood of the shelf; folded in on itself, betraying nothing of its contents.

With a shiver of inevitability, I entered the room and let the door click shut behind me. My fingers shook as I picked up the piece of paper. I held it at arm's length and walked stiffly to the bed. Then I sat down, unfolded it, and took a lungful of air.

> *So you think I've got personal baggage that's clouding my judgement and becoming a barrier to my performance? As for counselling, I'll be the one to decide if I need to see a shrink — no one else. Anyway, looks like I was just the warm-up act for the American. I can't stand watching you with him, and I'm not going to hang around while you turn me into your latest case study — so I'm going home. Don't bother trying to call me — I've already blocked your number.*

Dry-mouthed, I read it again and again — as if the words might change, a different meaning emerge . . . He'd got it completely wrong, of course — he was no warm-up act for anyone, least of all Troy. I had to find him, talk to him . . . Euston station, that was where he'd be; and trains to Manchester ran frequently — there was no time to lose.

Just as I reached the door, someone knocked — a loud knock, confident of an answer. My heart started to pound — he'd come back! I flung the door open, ready with a rueful smile.

But it wasn't Jack at all.

It was Troy, with a rueful smile of his own, arms spread in a gesture of reconciliation — even as his gaze sidestepped mine to survey the room behind me. I had no doubt that he was checking whether anyone else was there, and my lips set in a grim line.

I said coldly, 'How did you know where I was?'

'I got rid of Di and followed you.' His voice was soft and mild-mannered, recalling his first words to me earlier: *What an unexpected pleasure! At least, it's a pleasure for me. Let's hope you can say the same*. But I wasn't deceived: this was a surface civility, from a man brimming with negative emotion — and I represented the ideal outlet.

He went on, 'Can I come in, honey?'

'No.' I braced my body across the threshold, one hand gripping the door handle, the other clutching the security chain, still on its hook; too late to use it now. 'What do you want?'

'A chance to explain.'

A bitter little laugh. 'You had your chance three years ago, in another hotel bedroom — remember?'

'Oh, Aleesha.' The way he said my name — half sigh, half groan — spun like a stone into a pool of memories . . .

Get a grip, get a grip. 'Over here it's 'Alicia', if you don't mind.'

'Of course . . . *Aleesha*.' Before I could protest, he cupped my face in his hands; I tried to pull back, but he was too strong. 'In that other hotel bedroom, did you really think it was that simple?'

'Yes, until then I thought it was very simple. I was unattached, you acted like you were. We were in love — at least, *I* was — and I believed we had a future together. You said so yourself, many times.' I bit my lip, as if to stem the flow of recriminations. 'Now let go of me.'

'By the way,' he said, in a light, almost conversational tone, 'that was a great performance back there in the panel discussion. You took me by surprise, I was expecting to wipe the floor with you.' A low chuckle. 'You're blushing. I forgot, you never could cope with compliments. Remember what I said after our first night together?'

'No.'

'I said — '

'I don't want to hear it!'

'Okay, so you don't wanna hear it — but you can't take away the memories.' His thumbs shifted to either side of my mouth, mimicking their old tenderness. Once, this had been a cue to kiss. I swallowed — and immediately realised that his fingers would sense the movement of my throat; he would *know* that I remembered and, if I gave him the opportunity, he would use that knowledge . . .

I forced the coldness back into my voice. 'I'm working on that, believe me.'

His thumbs began their barely perceptible stroking. 'It might do you good to revisit them, one way or another.'

'No thanks, I've moved on.'

He smiled thinly. 'The big guy at the back of the room in the blue check shirt, right? I noticed how he couldn't take his eyes off you — or me. Wonder if he guessed who I was.'

'Why would he? You're hardly our number one topic of conversation.'

'But something rattled him.' His gaze strayed briefly along the corridor, as if distracted by a noise or movement, then returned. He said, almost casually, 'Where is he now?'

An air of bravado. 'In the bathroom.

You've got three seconds to get your hands off me before I call him.'

'Long enough for this?' Without waiting for an answer, he bent his head and kissed me. Not that I co-operated; I was too busy flexing my knee, preparing to deliver a short, sharp blow to his groin.

Then, out of nowhere, Jack's voice, icily clear: 'I thought I'd left something behind. But I haven't. I can see that now.'

The blood drained from my face. I tore myself away from guarding the door and pushed at Troy with both hands. A brief struggle as he resisted — but it was more for balance than control.

Because the damage was done. The timing of his kiss had been perfect: he'd seen Jack coming, he'd known I was bluffing, and he'd delivered one last malevolent blow.

I wrenched myself free, only to see Jack walking away. '*Jack!* It's not what you think!' It was little more than a croak, but he would have heard me. He *must* have heard me. Whereas seconds earlier I hadn't heard him at all, not even the pad of his footsteps on the deep, duplicitous carpet.

I made to go after him, but Troy grabbed my arm. I jerked round. 'Get off!'

His eyes bored into me. 'I don't recall you fighting like that for me.' His face, his tone — everything about him radiated resentment. Strange, wasn't it, when he'd just scored one final victory?

'Don't you remember?' A brittle smile. 'There wasn't anything to fight for, you'd already made your choice. I'll never forget the look on your face when Maria walked in.'

'I've told you — it wasn't as simple as that. Why won't you let me explain?' His shoulders slumped, as if in defeat; he said, with a mournful sigh, 'If it's any consolation, there are still places in California I can't bring myself to visit, thanks to you.'

A twinge of compassion for the man

from the Golden State, with his mantra of self-indulgence. I said, more gently than I'd intended, 'This is goodbye, Troy.' When I pulled away, he made no move to stop me. Not even when I swept past him into the room and slammed the door shut.

No point in going after Jack now; he's had too much of a head start. And I need some time alone. Time to recover from the events of the last few hours. Time to reflect on the future.

I leaned back against the door, drained; yet, at heart, calmer than I'd felt for years.

Only then did it hit me. I'd closed down this long-running chapter of my life — but at what cost to the next?

15

The first thing I did was run a bath, as if tempting fate; but there was no repeat of the night before. Not that I expected it. And perhaps, like other first times, it could never really be repeated.

As I lay shrouded in bubbles, I forced myself to confront my feelings for Troy in uncomfortable detail. Funny how a comparatively short episode could have had such a lasting impact. Less than two months of uninhibited hedonism — or, as he'd called it, total immersion — had resulted in three years of withdrawal into a half-life of restraint.

I resolved to shed the last vestiges of bitterness and self-reproach. As with any relationship, there were good memories mixed with the bad; with new insight, I realised that I just needed to give myself permission to enjoy them. After all, there were plenty to choose from . . . Walking in the National Redwood Forest, craning our necks at the trees; humbled — yes, even Troy had used the word — by their unearthly grandeur. Wine-tasting in Sonoma, Napa's quieter neighbour; his wry comment that we were already intoxicated by each other, a wine that money couldn't buy. Seeing the quirkiness of San Francisco through his eyes, from the brassy bustle of Fisherman's Wharf to the laid-back legacy of Haight-Ashbury's Summer of Love. Watching sunsets from his car, with its scents of leather and pine. And far more intimate recollections . . .

Why would I want to deny the episode, or — worse still — forget it? It had happened, deepened my experience of life, formed the person I was today.

The bubbles started to fade, exposing my arms. I noticed faint red fingerprints where Troy had grabbed me; and the angrier mark underneath, where he'd dug his nail into my skin. Difficult to reconcile this display of aggression with the man I'd known, and with the memories I'd just been rediscovering. Except that perhaps it pointed to some sort of inner turmoil, stirred up by seeing me again.

Of course I had older, deeper wounds; but they were psychological and self-inflicted. And the fact that they were at last starting to heal was largely down to my feelings for someone else. I squeezed my eyes tightly shut, battling a rush of emotion. Somewhere on a nearby street, a table for two was reserved in the name of Jack Smith: a poignant symbol of what might have been, but was now in jeopardy.

Could I make things right between us? I forced my analytical mind to summarise what I knew about him. He was a man who responded to actions more than words, whose personal loyalties were strong, but who was still working through the fallout from his father's death. His long-term relationship with fellow sufferer Karina, instead of helping, had intensified feelings of guilt and inadequacy — perhaps for both of them. Yet he had co-operated surprisingly well with my coaching offer of rapport, openness and trust: responding to the deep dive requests, sharing the tragic story of his father, respecting the rules I'd put in place between us — until I broke them.

Now, in whatever capacity — whether as his coach, friend, or lover — it seemed I had let him down. Which meant that I believed him when he said that he'd already blocked my mobile phone number. I needed to understand his reasons for leaving, and in return I needed a chance to explain.

A chance to explain . . . That had been Troy's request earlier, and I'd refused point blank. What if Jack did the same to me? I couldn't blame him for it. Bad enough that he'd felt somehow betrayed and walked out in the first place; even worse that he'd apparently changed his mind and returned, only to find me with Troy. Correction: to find me being kissed by Troy, without any obvious resistance. Jack had reacted with what I recognised as fight-or-flight, an acute stress response to a threat — either perceived or real. Now I needed to convince him that the attempted kiss belonged to the first category, not the second.

But he was on a train back to Manchester while I was still in London. A North-South divide that, at this moment, felt even wider than two hundred miles . . .

I got out of the bath and wrapped myself in a towel, debating whether to get dressed and go home; eventually, however, I secured the door and slipped between the sheets. They were cool and unwelcoming, so different from last night. Yet I decided to stay in the hotel as planned, sleep in the bed we'd shared. Not because I expected him to come back, but because I could pretend he was still here.

I lay still, while my mind raced through a plan of action. The best way — the only way — to explain everything was face to face; I reached for my phone and looked up the timetable for trains to Manchester. The first one in the morning was shortly after eight o'clock — I could get a taxi to Grimshaw, as I'd done on my last visit. Stupid thought. He'd hardly be at the office on a Sunday — and I had no idea where else to find him.

There was always Midge and Bill. Could I ask them to phone him and suggest lunch — Corleone's perhaps — so that I could turn up in their place? But that would mean taking them into my confidence; in which case I might as well abandon my play-acting and ask point blank where he lived.

Except the only contact information I had for Midge and Bill was a postal address.

I searched the online phone book, but could find no McGraws listed in Threlkeld; they must be ex-directory. I chewed my lip; how could I reach them, short of getting a taxi to Blencathra Lodge from the nearest station? And then it came to me — Midge and her paintings. I typed in 'Midge McGraw, artist', clicked on the first link that returned and almost whooped with delight. Her work was featured on a regional arts and crafts website, and her details included an email address that looked like a personal one.

It took a ridiculously long time to compose a short message:

Dear Midge,
I need to talk to you — tonight, if possible. Please could you send me the best contact number?
With kind regards,
Alicia

There, it was done; I just had to hope that she was someone who checked her emails regularly. I scrambled out of bed and made a cup of tea. Another reminder of the night before, and Jack's voice: *Got anything stronger?* I chose peppermint, in an attempt to hold onto my hard-won serenity.

My phone pinged. I snatched it up,

saw that Midge had replied and dialed her number — before I could change my mind.

She answered on the second ring. 'Alicia?'

'Yes. Sorry to bother you, it's just — ' I hesitated, unsure how much to tell.

'Is it about Jack?'

'Yes, I need to — oh Midge, I don't know where to start.'

'Why not at the beginning?'

I carried the cup of tea to the bedside table and settled myself against the pillows, on the side where he'd slept. *Deep breath — stay calm*. 'It depends which beginning you mean. The imaginary one, when we told you we'd met at the ballet — or the real one, when I went to his office on an executive coaching assignment.'

After that, it all spilled out. The instant attraction, and my refusal to acknowledge it . . . The complicated legacy of my relationship with Troy . . . My reluctant agreement to start the coaching . . . The suggested role play in the Lakes, and Jack's list of justifications . . . The realisation that a different agenda was emerging . . . Our separate decisions to bring the coaching to an end . . . His surprise trip to London, and its natural outcome . . . My surprise meeting with Troy, and its unintended consequences.

'I'm sorry for deceiving you and Bill,' I went on. 'But, whatever you think of me, please help me to make things right with Jack. I want to go and see him tomorrow — except I haven't a clue where he lives.'

Silence; then she said drily, 'I'm tempted to take you there myself — but only so that I can kill him with my bare hands, and that would defeat the whole object of your visit.'

'I'm sorry.'

'You've nothing to be sorry about, whereas he . . . ' Her voice trailed away. 'It's true that Bill and I assumed from the way he talked that you were his girlfriend. And it would certainly have been a good tactic with Karina, if she'd bothered to turn up. But there was no need to keep the coaching under wraps — Bill would have told you what you wanted to know, he'd do anything for Jack.'

I digested this in silence. Even though Midge had confirmed two of Jack's reasons for the role play, she was still baffled by the third reason — the one most closely related to my coaching assignment, the one I should have rejected on the spot. Why had I allowed myself to be persuaded so easily into the role of Jack's girlfriend? Could it be because, subconsciously, I was already half in love with him? And all the time I thought myself immune, because he reminded me of Troy . . .

They're not really alike, of course — Jack's a far better man. It was more my reactions to him that brought back memories of Troy — something I should have realised right from the start. But that doesn't change the fact that I could have interviewed Bill openly . . .

'I see,' I managed at last. 'Well, you

can take me to his house, but it sounds like I should be the one killing him with my bare hands. As slowly and painfully as possible.'

She laughed. 'Och, I don't think he's in any real danger from either of us, is he? But I'm serious about the first part of the offer, I could meet you somewhere near Manchester. Are you driving, or coming by train?'

'Train. If I go home to get my car, I might chicken out.'

'Can you get to Preston station, then? Saves me negotiating Manchester city centre, and Jack's only half an hour or so from there.'

It was arranged in a moment; I would get the first direct train from Euston, arriving shortly before noon. She and Bill would pick me up and drive me to Jack's house — and that was as far as the plan went. I shied away from any further discussion, and she didn't encourage me.

We ended the call with profuse thanks on my side, and cheerful protests on hers. Alone with my thoughts once again, I sipped my tea, besieged by regret and uncertainty. I longed for, yet dreaded, tomorrow — knowing that, once I saw Jack, I would be either elated or distraught. And, right now, it was too close to call. In the end I fell into an exhausted sleep, and dreamt that I went to Jack's house. I rang the bell, but it was Karina who came to the door . . .

Morning broke, relentless sunshine. I got up too soon, packed too quickly, checked out of the hotel and arrived half an hour early for my train. I spent most of this time agonising over which ticket to buy. A day return was too restrictive, given that I had no guarantee of Jack being at home, and might even have to wait until he showed up at work. An open return seemed to demonstrate a reluctance to commit, a triumph of the rational over the emotional. I opted — with a thrill of trepidation — for a single: no limitation on the date, or even the starting point of my return to the south.

Once on the train, I bought a

newspaper and a coffee, and went through the motions of enjoying both. I felt that, if I analysed or prepared in any way for what was to come, I would fail. *For the first time since that Californian summer, I'm being led by my heart as opposed to my head. Scary.*

Reading a paper wouldn't normally fill a journey of almost three hours; but fortunately this was a Sunday, and there was a seemingly endless supply of newsprint. At last I heard the announcement that Preston would be the next stop. *Deep breath. And another.*

I texted Midge to say that I'd arrived, and received an instant reply: 'Am outside — you can't miss me!' I marched through the ticket barrier, fabricating a smile at the same railway official who'd helped me a week ago — and then hesitated outside the station, unsure which of the parked cars to head for. There weren't many to choose from: a battered silver people carrier, a small yellow hatchback, an old white van — no, a motorhome. A motorhome that looked vaguely, heart-stoppingly, familiar.

The nut-brown arm waggling out of the driver's window settled it. As I approached, Midge jumped down and gave me a hug.

'No hard feelings?' I said, shyly.

She picked up my case and stowed it in the luggage compartment. 'No hard feelings at all, and Bill's the same. He's gone on ahead, by the way — he wanted to check out the lie of the land at Jack's.'

I puzzled over her last comment as I swung myself up into the passenger seat. 'Why aren't you travelling together?'

She didn't answer immediately; once the engine spluttered into life, she concentrated on manoeuvring Hermann into the sporadic flow of traffic. Then, with an apologetic smile, 'We decided you needed a back-up plan. After we drop you at Jack's, we'll be skedaddling off home — but if we leave Hermann behind then you can camp out on his doorstep in comfort.'

I suppressed a gulp of dismay. 'Do

you think that's going to be necessary?'

'Who knows? He may be out until this evening, or he may not want to co-operate — at least at first,' she added, hastily. 'Anyway, I thought you liked Hermann?'

'I do, I really do. I'm just a bit on edge about how Jack's going to react. Any advice? You know him so much better than I do.'

'In some ways.' She waved vigorously at a motorhome coming the other way.

'Friends of yours?'

She laughed. 'No, it's what we do in the motorhome community, wave to each other on the road. Just like we give our motorhomes proper names, like Hermann. Back to your question. Yes, I've got some advice for you.' A sideways look at me. 'Decide what you want out of your relationship with Jack, and go for it. No more pussyfooting around.'

I was silent. Then, with a forced laugh, 'That's sort of what I tell my coaching clients. It starts with goal-setting, but then there's always the deep dive — the reality check. I know what my goal is with Jack, what I don't know is how realistic it is. And there's no time to do the deep dive justice.'

Another motorhome, another wave from Midge. 'You know, Alicia, you can plan your life as much as you want, but it'll always throw you a curved ball at some time or other. It's how you deal with the unexpected, or the unknown, that matters.'

She was right, of course. Which was why my comfort zone was executive coaching, with its focus on business. Somehow that applied an order — albeit a superficial one — to the natural chaos of human needs and emotions and communications.

She went on, 'Anyway, wasn't last weekend the deep dive with Jack? Pretending to be in love by day, and sharing a rather cramped space by night — you couldn't help getting to know him better, surely?'

I swallowed and stared out of the window. We were driving through a landscape of moors and scattered cottages; bleaker than the Lakes, with only a smudge of hills in the distance. 'Are we nearly there?' My voice was little more than a whisper.

'Ten minutes to Ramsbottom,' she said, as if that explained everything. She added, gently, 'If it's any consolation, based on what I saw, I think you and Jack do have a future together.' Just as I was about to ask her to elaborate, her mobile rang. 'That'll be Bill. Can you speak to him? I'm not hands free.'

I cleared my throat and took the call. Bill was phoning to report that Jack's car was nowhere to be seen, and to suggest lunch in one of the local pubs. I relayed this message to Midge and she nodded. 'Tell him to try the Eagle and Child first — we'll be there in ten.'

The houses were clustered more densely now, suggesting some form of village or town. At first glance, their old stone walls glowed with the mellowness of those in the south; but I detected a darker hue, as if the soot of Victorian industry still lingered. Attractive, though, and in keeping with the wilder landscape.

The pub was one of the larger buildings, and inside everything was clean and bright and shining. The warmth of Bill's welcome, the cosy table for three, and the impressive Sunday lunch helped me to relax — once I'd stopped watching the door, in case Jack walked in.

We left an hour and a half later, setting off in convoy back the way we'd come. After a mile or two, we turned off the main road and into a narrow street. At the end, backing onto the moors, was a row of six old cottages, huddled together in pairs. Midge pulled up outside the furthest one, where the road broadened out to allow parking for several cars. Jack's was not among them.

'That's his house, the one with the blue door,' she said. 'I'll show you where everything is in here, then Bill and I will be heading off.'

My stomach churned in disbelief; despite her earlier warning, I'd been fooling myself that they'd still be around when Jack returned — to act as referees, perhaps. I stood as if in a trance while she retrieved my suitcase, produced a mug, tea and some milk, explained the idiosyncrasies of the plumbing. Then she handed me the keys and hugged me goodbye.

I blinked rapidly. 'But how will I get Hermann back to you?' I said, knowing that this was the least of my worries.

'Och, we'll think of something. Now you make yourself a nice cuppa and wait for Jack.' She cocked her head on one side, as if noting my agitation for the first time. 'Do you want me to ring him and find out when he'll be coming home? I'm sure I can think of an excuse to be in touch.'

'No thanks,' I said, forcing a smile. 'For once in my life, I'd rather not be prepared.'

16

When they'd gone, I kicked off my shoes and sat on the bed, leaning back against the cushions. From here, through the window with its cheerful red curtains, I had a good view of Jack's cottage. It looked well-kept — the paintwork new, the garden tidy — and I liked the style, more workmanlike than chocolate-box. I wondered how long he'd lived here, how much it was troubled by memories of Karina, whether I'd ever have the opportunity to displace them. I must have been so absorbed in my thoughts that I didn't hear the approach of a car. It was only when the door of the motorhome swung open that I realised he'd returned. As he saw me, I watched his expression flick from friendly curiosity to barely contained anger.

'What the — ?' He stepped inside

and, as always, the motorhome seemed to shrink. 'God knows how you got here — well, I can guess — but it won't do any good.'

Not the start I'd been hoping for. I said, as evenly as I could, 'We need to have a proper talk, and I'm not leaving until we do.'

'Then you'll be here a very long time.' His face radiated hostility, his tone was curt — as if there'd never been anything between us.

'I'll wait,' I said, crossing my arms.

He frowned. 'Where are Midge and Bill? They must have had a hand in this.'

'On their way home. Yes, they've been very helpful, even after they found out about our little deception last weekend.' A wry smile. 'I was astonished to learn that Bill would have been fine about talking to me as your coach. Instead, we had to go along with your ridiculous plan — '

'My plan was for public performances only, not that I'd need the willpower of a saint. I meant it when I said you'd be safe with me. I didn't know we'd be shacked up together in the same bed, I thought we'd get away with separate rooms, remember?'

'So why did you *really* want them to think I was your girlfriend?'

He took a couple of paces towards me. A shaft of sunlight glinted through the window onto his face, accentuating its angles and shadows; more of them than usual, as if he hadn't slept all night. Yet, when he looked at me, something flickered in his eyes — then he blinked and glanced away. Rightly or wrongly, what I interpreted as desperation gave me hope.

'If you must know,' he said, staring down at the floor, 'it was to prove a point about *us*. Bill was just the easiest way of getting through your defences.'

My lips tightened. 'And what point was that?'

His head jerked up. 'You don't need me to tell you that, surely? It was obvious to me from the moment we met that we both . . . that what happened on Friday night was just a matter of time.' It was the black-velvet voice, but rubbed the wrong way.

Had I been that transparent? Maybe he knew I was in love with him even before I knew myself. Maybe the role play was simply a test, to see how far I'd go. Did I pass — or did I fail? To cover my confusion, I got up from the bed and twitched the duvet straight, tears stinging at the back of my eyes. He was close enough to notice, if he wanted to; but I didn't care — I had nothing more to lose.

'So is that it?' I said, dully. 'You've proved your point, had your fun and it's time to move on?'

'Isn't that what you've just done? Slept with me one night, that American bastard the next — '

I lunged at him, hand raised. 'How *dare* you!' The adrenaline ebbed, and I slowly lowered my arm. 'If you'd stuck around long enough, you'd have known that didn't happen.'

He didn't seem to be listening. 'What's that?' He took hold of my wrist, surprisingly gentle, turning it over to examine the punctured skin. 'It wasn't there before.'

I swallowed. 'Troy did it, accidentally, during the panel discussion.'

'Accidentally or not, if he was here now I'd punch his lights out.' His grip tightened imperceptibly, while our eyes met. For the first time since he'd arrived, neither of us looked away.

Deep breath. 'Jack, please let me explain about him.'

'You don't have to.' His mouth twisted into a grimace. 'It was obvious from everything he said — everything he did — who he was, what you'd been to each other. And when I changed my mind and came back — there he was, all over you — '

'He knew you were there and made it look as if we were kissing — but we weren't. I got rid of him a few minutes later and I haven't seen him since. I don't want — I've *never* wanted

— anything more to do with him.' My voice faltered, in spite of — or perhaps because of — a desperate need to convince him; I stumbled on, the final confession. 'But until I met you, I hadn't realised how much he was still in my system. Like a poison — and you're the antidote. You've got to believe me — please.'

Silence, while I watched the struggle in his face: head against heart, past against future, doubt against trust. A struggle that, in recent weeks, had become all too familiar for me, too. At last he said quietly, 'I'm doing my best.'

Then he lifted my wrist and pressed his lips to the red mark. A small gesture, yet hugely significant. I held my breath and waited.

With great deliberation, he released my arm, placed his hands on my hips and drew me close, his gaze steady and direct. 'You see, that argument between you and the American, about ethics and boundaries, it really got to me. I started to doubt all the good things that had happened between us . . . And I got angry, when I should have been sorry.'

My eyes widened. 'Sorry? Whatever for?'

'Always pushing you to be less professional and more personal — and then the role play.' A weary-sounding sigh. 'That could have been a disaster, I just didn't think — '

'Except it wasn't a disaster, for either of us.' A tremulous smile. 'And now that we don't have a professional relationship, there's no conflict of interest. I could be your girlfriend in a heartbeat.'

'A heartbeat? I was hoping it wouldn't take that long.' Then he bent his head and kissed me; light, brushing kisses on the mouth, each one more lingering than the last — a perfect blend of passion and affection.

I think — I know *— this means that everything's going to be all right.*

When the kisses stopped, we linked hands — as though, now that we were reconciled, we couldn't bear to break the physical connection.

'How long can you stay?' he said, softly.

It was tempting to say, 'Forever'; but I confined myself to the short term. 'I have a meeting tomorrow afternoon — shall I make it a conference call?'

'Definitely. And then?'

An airy shrug, designed to tease. 'Oh, I'm between clients, and the last one was particularly troublesome — so I think I'm entitled to some time off. What about you?'

A wide, wicked, wonderful grin. 'Oh, I'm between coaches, and the last one was — ouch!' — as I used our joined hands to prod him in the ribs — 'a real handful.' He slipped his other hand inside my shirt. 'Still is, in fact. Plus I need to get into training for the World Black Pudding Throwing Championship — '

'You're kidding — aren't you?'

'Nope, it takes place in Ramsbottom every September and I usually start my preparation about now. So I think I'm entitled to some time off, too.'

I giggled. 'Are you comparing me to a black pudding?'

'If I was, it would be a very interestingly shaped one.'

'Is that the best you can do — 'interestingly?' Not much of a compliment.'

'Okay, then — *beautifully* shaped.' He removed his hand from inside my shirt and tilted my face up to his. 'If I can clear my diary, shall we go back to the Lakes?'

'You mean take Hermann home?'

'I don't think he deserves to go home just yet, do you? Maybe we could go the long way round to Threlkeld, walk up some of the western fells, the ones we saw from Latrigg.'

'I'd like that.' From outside came the muffled slam of a car door; over his shoulder, I watched a grey-haired woman walk briskly up to the cottage with the blue door. 'Are you expecting a visitor?'

He turned his head to follow my gaze. 'Uh-oh, that's my mother. Still, I suppose you'll have to meet sometime.'

I stared at him in alarm. 'You'd better go and talk to her while I — no, wait!' With panicking fingers, I adjusted my shirt, smoothed my hair. 'Do I look presentable?'

He tucked a stray strand of hair behind my ear. 'You'll do,' he said, with what I hoped was typical northern understatement. 'Not that it matters. Once she's got over the fact that you were born south of Stockport, I'll mention the words 'marriage' and 'children' — and she won't care about anything else.'

He's going too far, too fast. And yet . . . it's a vision of our future together that, amazingly, I can relate to completely. Is there a catch somewhere? I can't see one, unless —

'Jack, please say this is *not* another role play.'

He smiled and said, 'This is for real, Alicia. This is for real.'

Thank You

Hello

Thank you for reading my book. I hope you enjoyed Alicia and Jack's journey — I certainly loved writing it. As with my other books, I looked to a 19th-century classic for inspiration — in this case, Elizabeth Gaskell's *North & South*. And it helped to watch the 2004 BBC adaptation a few times, too!

If you enjoyed meeting Alicia and Jack, please tell the world — or at least your nearest and dearest. The best way of doing this is to write an online review — it only takes a few moments, and I'd love to hear what you thought. Reviews (especially the ones with lots of stars) inspire authors like me to keep writing, and our publishers to keep supporting us.

One Summer Weekend is essentially Alicia's story. I'd like to tell Jack's, too. Watch out for the next instalment!

Juliet

X

Other titles in the Linford Romance Library:

THE LEGACY OF BLACKTHORN

June Davies

During a stormy winter's night, Meirian Penlan travels by stagecoach to take up a mysterious post at Blackthorn Manor. Wild and remote, Blackthorn lies amongst the great meres of Lancashire, surrounded by long-held superstitions, tales of witchcraft and uncanny occurrences. Once there, Meirian is drawn into a web of scandal, deception, blackmail and tragedy. Discovering old love letters and a terrible secret, she risks everything to set right a dreadful wrong — and unravel the disappearance of Blackthorn's medieval jewels . . .

LEXIE'S UNFORESEEN BENEFACTOR

Eileen Knowles

Twenty-year-old Lexie fears their family-run hotel may be heading for bankruptcy due to her mismanagement. She doesn't know which way to turn when, out of the blue, her father and his stepson Jake get in touch. Lexie had always thought her father was dead, and is startled by his sudden appearance, while Jake proves to be more than a little intimidating. When he offers a way out of her financial problems, Lexie reluctantly accepts, only to discover how authoritarian he can be . . .